Laura

La cigogne du marché de Noël

Tristan Mieger

Illustré par Samy El Hamlili

Dans le cœur tranquille de
Strasbourg,

Où les maisons à colombages peintes
dans des teintes
vibrantes bercent de charmantes rues
pavées,

Vivait une cigogne nommée Laura.

Contrairement à ses congénères qui, à l'approche de l'hiver, s'envolent vers les vents du sud,

Laura affiche un audacieux défi. Elle décida résolument de rester, ses yeux curieux aspirant à voir la ville sous un manteau de neige immaculée.

Et à assister au déroulement de l'envoûtant marché de Noël.

Alors que les premiers flocons
commencent à tomber

Et que les autres cigognes s'envolent
vers des
territoires plus chauds,

Laura se retrouve **seule**.
Les nids autrefois animés sur les toits
de Strasbourg
étaient froids et déserts.

Affamée et grelottante,

Elle se demande comment elle va
survivre à l'hiver qui s'annonce.

Pourtant, le moral au beau fixe,
elle décide de braver l'aventure.

Alors que les jours sont de plus en plus courts et froids,

Laura trouve refuge en se perchant sur la
haute flèche de la cathédrale de Strasbourg.

De là, elle a une vue plongeante sur la ville, observant
les chemins pavés se transformer en
une mosaïque de blanc et les lumières
scintillantes du marché

L'arôme des marrons grillés et du vin chaud monte jusqu'à son perchoir et fait gargouiller son estomac.

À la recherche de nourriture, Laura se retrouve à planer au-dessus du marché,

Ses yeux perçants scrutant la foule

Elle aperçoit une vieille femme à l'air aimable qui vend du pain d'épice.

Tentant sa chance, elle descendit en piqué, prit un pain d'épice et remonta rapidement dans le ciel.

La femme lève les yeux, d'abord surprise,

Puis son étonnement se transforme en un sourire chaleureux lorsqu'elle voit Laura disparaître dans le ciel enneigé.

Une amitié unique est née, et chaque jour, la femme laisse un peu de pain à Laura.

Lorsque les premiers bourgeons du printemps sont apparus et que les autres cigognes sont revenues,

Elles ont trouvé Laura non seulement vivante, mais prospère.

Avec des yeux émerveillés, elles écoutent ses récits sur la ville enneigée,

Sur le marché de Noël enchanteur, sur ses amitiés improbables,

Le tout sous le regard attentif de l'imposante cathédrale.

Ainsi, alors qu'ils se délestaient des récits de leur voyage vers le sud,

Laura se tenait debout et fière.

Son histoire était **différente**, remplie de défis et de triomphes propres à son

© 2023, Coronelle Editions et Productions, 2 rue de l'école Herrlisheim

Imprimé en France

Printed in Great Britain
by Amazon

34640178R00016

3   £1-50

CW00662614

SCARECROWS
DON'T MOVE

A Kate Taylor Crime Thriller

by Jack Kale

To those who fight child abuse in all its forms throughout the world.

"We must not make a scarecrow of the law, setting it up to fear the birds of prey, and let it keep one shape till custom make it their perch and not their terror."

WILLIAM SHAKESPEARE

SCARECROWS
DON'T MOVE

A Kate Taylor Crime Thriller

by Jack Kale

CONTENTS

1. Morning Has Broken

Today would be interesting, but first she would need to settle her stomach and get rid of the headache. Kate Taylor stepped out of her kimono into the shower. She breathed out deeply under the soothing stream of warm water cascading through her dark, shoulder length hair.

The paracetamol was beginning to have the desired effect and Kate just hoped there would be a nice sausage roll and some "Pepsi" in the fridge. As a hangover cure she swore by those two things, she had done ever since her university days.

Sundays were supposed to be her chilling day. Lounge around in oversized harem pants and floppy jumpers, read a book, sip some wine and nibble your way through the fridge. Inevitably this followed on from an 'anything goes' Saturday. This weekend it hadn't quite worked out that way. Sunday had been hijacked and had gone the same way as a Saturday. The good news, she hadn't dragged anyone back from the pub with her this time, no uncomfortable explanations required, no awkward and clumsy scene involving an attempt to get dressed in front of a vaguely remembered male form, no attempting to slip into knickers in a classy way. Such a "way" just didn't exist. No meaningless goodbyes, exaggerated performance ratings, and no pointless swapping of telephone numbers.

Kate noticed she was humming to herself. Something from one of the band's better songs. They had performed last night with passion and enthusiasm, but lacking any real content, catchy tune though.

'Not a good move,' muttered Kate to herself. 'An early morning meeting with the boss and you go on the red stuff. Still not the first time and it sure won't be the last.'

She pulled together what threads of her fogged senses she could and gave some thought to the day ahead. What to wear? Kate knew there was no point in even considering the outcome of this particular issue, it would be the black skirt, black jacket, white blouse and of course black shoes, but hey, the bright red lipstick was definitely coming out, a bit of white makeup under the eyes to ease out the knackered look.

Kate viewed herself in the full length mirror adorning her bedroom wall. She smiled, pleased with what she saw. 'Mid-forties and still got it girl.' She kept herself fit, needed to with the stresses and strains of her job. She was lean, her skin glowing, her body taut and lithe. The problem was, in her profession, she had to be more man than a woman, more Mike Tyson than Marilyn Monroe and that was something Kate Taylor could do.

For once the fridge came up trumps and Kate's "day after" remedy went down a treat. She noticed you just couldn't help but get crumbs of pastry down your front when you eat a sausage roll. Eating them in a car was worse, they seemed to turn up everywhere for the next couple of weeks until you had no choice but to hoover the damn thing from top to bottom. The Pepsi, that just gave you wind but it sure helped debloat the stomach.

Medicine out of the way and finally fully dressed, Kate checked her handbag, double locked the front door and slid into her car seat. The drive to the office always took an age, luckily the car seemed to know the way which meant Kate, could concentrate on the day ahead.

She knew it was going to be an interesting meeting just as she knew she was about to be 'kippered.' She had studiously read the files, their contents gave her little confidence in achieving the results that would be demanded from her new role. However, she liked the task they had lined up for her, it suited her. It was certainly an area she had longed to get her teeth into, she didn't however, relish having to work with a completely new team. Making a boat load of new people gel would take time, and she had a feeling time was not something she would get a lot of.

Car parked Kate entered the lift pressing the button for the fourth floor. It was like any other lift, a sticky carpet, buttons you don't really want to touch. Annoyingly it stopped at every floor on its slow ascent, as it always did. People stepped in, and they stepped out, and there were always a couple of idiots who wanted to go down, instead of up, getting into the lift, looking puzzled and then exiting with great haste to avoid embarrassment. No one talked. One or two shuffled, a stifled cough, a noise created by somebody's fingers doing something unnatural. She hated that cracking.

The time had come. Kate had to focus and that wouldn't be easy. She ran the gauntlet of a large open plan office and knocked on the frosted glass of a door that bore the name, and of course title, of the well renowned, and equally well loathed, DCS Jonathan Ratcliffe.

'Come in DI Taylor and take a seat. 'Coffee.' Kate declined the offer, it wouldn't sit well with the Pepsi.

'You know why we've chosen you don't you.'

It was a statement of fact not a question. Kate nibbled her lower lip, a habit she had perfected over the years, her way of counting to ten, her defensive wall to an ill-advised comment. It rarely worked.

She didn't answer, she couldn't answer because it was the wrong answer, not the one they wanted to hear, but she knew it to be the truth. She longed to just speak up. "Presumably it's because you think you might need a scapegoat Sir, if it goes arse up Sir, and I'm as good a scapegoat as you'll find around here."

Just for once the words were unspoken, she restrained herself, her thoughts remaining just that. Conflict was avoided, no more brownie points lost.

She noticed the sun glinting off the windows, the reflected frown on her face, the highly polished desk surface and the spick and span figure of her boss opposite her. She watched his annoying habit of twitching his nose whenever he sought an immediate answer. Kate was not going to humour him.

Detective Constable Superintendent Jonathan Ratcliffe put aside his increasing irritation at the woman opposite him. She never changed. Nobody liked working with her, well maybe a select few. He had tried, but when it came to officers like him, men like him, there was no getting through, no bypassing those steel bars wrapped tightly around her emotions. Kate Taylor, he knew was a cynic, but, he accepted, a damn good police officer. Totally focused, results driven, born to arrest people.

'And your team Kate, handpicked, although you will have the final say, of sorts.'

Her lower lip came in for some more punishment. 'I've read the dossiers Sir.'

'A good balance of experience and fresh eyes I think you will agree.'

Kate ran the information she had gleaned from her reading through her mind, once more choosing to remain silent, whilst "Politically correct is what you mean", were the words dangerously perched on her tongue. The files suggested a group of people more in line with the Magnificent Seven than the optimistic picture painted by her new boss.

Ratcliffe was nearing the end of his tether, which with Kate Taylor was proving to be rather short. He was looking forward to a cup of tea. 'Detective Sergeants Rashi Kamani and Eve Kendall come especially recommended. I am sure you will make a good team.'

Kate considered what they might have been recommended for and smirked, immediately regretting it.

'Did I say something amusing DI Taylor?' The meeting was getting edgy and Kate knew it was time to play the game. She could do that.

'Absolutely not Sir. I was just wandering what they were going to make of me, as I am sure they will have had plenty of officers offering their opinion.' Kate was also wondering which of the officers assigned to her would turn out to be the inevitable mole, placed in the team to report back to High Command. The one that at the end of the day would give the commanding officer his lifeline if things went badly.

'Unfortunately, I would have to agree with you.' The Chief Inspector smiled with what might have been taken as a genuine token of warmth, or at least a small and no doubt begrudging show of sympathy for her. It was neither. 'Kate make these people your own. We don't see eye to eye, but I have some respect for your achievements, and I know you do not let your colleagues down, ever. You may not be able to get them to love you but by God I know they are going to fear you. This 'mission' is made for you Kate, there are bastards out there causing pain, grief, despair and mental stress from which their victims rarely recover. Get them for me Kate!'

Kate would "get them" for herself, nobody else, but she felt now was the time to soften her approach. 'Thank you for the opportunity Sir. You are right this job is made for me and I will not be stopped from cracking heads and bringing these pathetic excuses for men to justice.'

DI Taylor your task is straight forward, track down the grooming gangs that we know are relentlessly abusing young girls. Your road ahead however is paved with obstacles that I fear you may not be able to overcome. The politics, the fear, the silence may yet defeat you in your pursuit of justice.'

'If I fail Sir, it won't be for the lack of trying.'

'Excellent your team will be waiting for you in two days' time. I believe you have one last date with your friends in the Drugs Squad.'

'Yes Sir. One final day of removing the scum of the earth from our streets Sir.'

Kate stood to leave.

One more thing, I expect daily reports and I mean daily.'

'Sir.' Kate opened the door and headed for her last drugs raid. 'Daily reports' she muttered. 'Written daily, read whenever.'

2. Final Fling

A thick set terrier, a black American Pit Bull, padded up the tree lined road. He had the look of violence about him. His owner had the same look, lean, hungry, cold. The air was crisp, the sky clear, the sun bright but cool. Meanwhile all around them, eyes watched, fingers twitched, boots creaked, nothing moved.

They stopped suddenly. A furtive glance preceded a deliberate diversion from their path into a narrow alley leading to a row of red brick houses. The door of the end property opened, the pair entered, a head peered out, looked both ways and disappeared.

Two more figures of equal height appeared from a nearby passageway. One received five crisp bank notes and left quickly, a smile on his face. Several more shadows began to move swiftly, quietly, threateningly forward, surrounding the property at the end of the row of houses. Their actions were deliberate, calm steps leading them to a planned encounter.

Radios crackled into life, four men moved to the front of the house. The "Enforcer", sixteen kilos of reinforced steel was about to be used to its usual devastating effect.

A woman moved deliberately forward from across the road to join the action. She arrived as the front door of the identified target burst open, the "Big Red Key" as it was known with affection by the force, having done its job.

The silence of the morning was shattered. Shots were fired from within, a stun grenade thrown in return. Shouting bounced around the walls of the building, adding its own sense of boding to the scene being enacted within. The shooting stopped, only the butcher's bill to tally.

The activity had been short, sharp, and cruel, and yet now a sense of stillness pervaded, adrenaline had risen and was now replaced by cool efficiency, and the job had been done.

'Great work guys.' Kate Taylor spoke to no one in particular but everyone who heard accepted the praise as if it were meant for them alone. The specialist team's leader strode up to his female colleague. 'Great haul in there Kate. Looks a shit hole from outside but there's got to be a high street value of at least a quarter of a million worth of powder in there. Shame it's your last bust for a while. It's always good working with you. Bit of a lucky mascot.'

'You're telling me George.' Kate viewed the carnage. Small scale this time but enough to make anyone shudder. 'Shouldn't be long before I'm back, probably with a demotion considering the can of worms they have thrown at me.'

George Mellor grimaced and placed a large calloused hand on her shoulder. At least a foot taller than Kate he peered down at her through his piercing blue eyes. 'Good luck from all of us. Don't be a stranger.'

Kate stared at him. 'Thanks. Now get your bloody huge paw off me and give me the basics to report back with.'

George laughed. Kate was not one to look down to in any shape or form. He accepted the rebuke, he wouldn't expect anything else from her. It had not been his intention to appear patronising, his actions were rather, a small show of peer affection.

'A couple of our boys with bruises, two suspects injured, requiring an ambulance, one destined for the morgue, plus of course an internal investigation as to why we shot him. After all he was only looking to give us a warm welcome, his shots merely a volley in celebration of our presence. Two more in custody and a load of social despair removed from our streets. How's that.'

'And the dog?'

'The bastard tried to bite Finney's leg, what do you think?'

It was Kate's turn to laugh. 'Your summary of events will do for me, but I would suggest you get somebody else to do the final draft if I were you. Reports never were your strong point, and DCI Kenny Turner might be flexible, but he certainly likes a good report.'

DI Taylor headed for her car still feeling the buzz a raid like this always created. She was certain she would be back with the Drug Squad, but for now, there was a different kind of evil to destroy, and she was the woman to do it.

'Why do all coppers love an Italian restaurant Kate?' DCI Kenny Turner was her boss and had requested the opportunity to say his farewell in a less formal way. He had some advice to impart, some thanks to convey, and a warning to serve. They sat at a small table in the corner of a very traditional eatery. Low ceilings discoloured by the years, a carpet, red mixed in with a fading palette of colours, garlic bulbs strategically placed, old wine bottles lining the walls.

'Come on Kenny most of them visit for the Peroni and limit their exploration of the menu to "spag bol" and pizza.'

'Good point. I guess I'm going to have to change my mind about what I was just about to order after that comment. Pretty much put me in my place.'

'Don't worry Kenny I won't think any worse of you than I already do. Go ahead, usual topping, chorizo, cheese and peppers, lots of them.'

'After what you said I think I'll add some olives just for a bit of a change, you might even say a slice of excitement.' Kate groaned.

'Are you ready to order some drinks?' They were interrupted

by Emilio who even at the age of seventy had the Italian knack of looking and sounding seductive. He was tall and despite being surrounded all day long by the best food money can buy, he was slim, retaining a wonderfully healthy texture to his smooth olive hued skin. He had owned the restaurant named after him for over forty years and he and his wife still ruled the roost.

'It has to be Chianti doesn't it Kate?' The two police officers had spent many a night at Emilio's usually celebrating a successful operation. Tonight was different. For one thing it wasn't exactly a celebration, each of them wary of the future for different reasons, one of which would become apparent later in the evening

'Classico?' Emilio had an exceptionally large selection of Chianti's and this first question could be succeeded by so many more.'

'As long as it has a cockerel on the bottle neck it will be fine.'

Emilio grinned he had enjoyed his fun. Tonight was busy so he abandoned his famously long chat lines and headed off to find one of the best of his bottles for one of his most favourite of customers.

They settled down and the conversation flowed. As usual they reminisced over the funnier things that had happened during their time on the "squad".

Kenny had just finished repeating his favourite stories about some of the stupid places drugs dealers hid their stash, particularly those that insisted on attempting to hide it on and within their bodies, when Emilio arrived with the main dish. 'For you Kate "Alla Panna", ham, mushrooms and our delicious white wine sauce served with tortellini. Absolutely delicious, tonight more so than ever, my wife has excelled herself yet again.' Emilio's mouth was watering his appreciation of Kate's choice more than apparent. 'And pizza.' He smiled broadly at Kate. 'The usual, with olives.' He looked disparagingly at Kenny, put his nose in the air and departed for the kitchen, laughing all the way.

'He certainly knows how to put you in your place doesn't he,' said Kenny.

Kate nodded in agreement. 'I love him to bits, great sense of humour and his wife is a real treasure. Long may they reign.'

They were halfway through their meal and Kenny decided there would never be a good time to give Kate his news. He was well aware that once delivered it would almost certainly take quite a while to talk things through, and so with a deep breath he approached the subject he was dreading.

'Kate I'm not sure if you are aware but Frank Moon was released today.' Kenny let the news sink in. Kate continued chewing, her reaction imperceptible. She swallowed a mouthful of wine, sat back, chewed her bottom lip, and looked long and hard at her boss. 'And?' It was a show of bravado, they both recognised it as such. Kate sighed.

'You put him away Kate, I just thought you should know. Probably not an issue but as you very well know, every now and again one of these bastards decides he deserves a little dose of revenge. If this one does, I am very aware you are not going to be in the midst of your tried and trusted team and as such you could be more exposed than normal to any danger that may or may not exist.'

Kate knew the score. It was one of the hazards of the job and not often but every now and again one of these morons got lucky and a cop got hurt. 'I'll keep alert boss.'

'Please do Kate. Be very assured, we will be keeping tabs on him for a good while just to be on the safe side. If we have any concerns your protection will be paramount, and we will be there. Now what advice can I give you to help you in your new role?'

Kate pondered the question. 'Listen Kenny you will be the first person I call if I get stuck. Now let's talk about something far more important to a girl.'

'Pudding?'

'In one.'

3. First Impressions

'Good morning, I am DI Kate Taylor. Congratulations you have the misfortune of being selected to be part of my team. Does anyone here know what that team is tasked with?' She was buzzing, she had to be. Leadership relied on confidence, which in turn was built on adrenalin. She had undergone her "Bruce Forsyth pre meeting" routine, designed to set her levels of perceived commitment at a high level. It involved smashing sheets of rolled up paper against a wall or desk whilst proclaiming 'I am going to be great, great, great.' It was a good routine as long as nobody walked into the washroom at the wrong time. On those occasions it was a touch embarrassing.

The complete silence emanating from the group confirmed they didn't know, or at least at this stage, wanted one of the others to answer. Kate had already decided she would hit them with the sledgehammer. 'What I am about to tell you will lead you to decide whether to stay or go. Please do either with my full support, but please note, if you stay you are mine to do with as I think fit. I will not be nice, I will not be sympathetic, I will not be your token mother. I will be fair and reasonable, most importantly I will have your backs. You in turn will have mine and be ready to die, if not for me, then most certainly for the people we intend to protect.

I have a few rules. Number one if you have something to say, say it, no backstabbing, no bad mouthing of me or of each other. Step out of line on this and you will be gone, no second chance, good riddance. Second speak plainly, speak openly. If you want to express an opinion do so, you never know it might be helpful. Feel free to criticise myself or any member of the team, but only in private team meetings and only if you add the word "because" to your criticism.

Number three. I do not like swearing. Do not swear unnecessarily anywhere, anytime that I am around. If you are in mortal danger or extreme pain, please feel free to ignore this rule. Four we can do away with officialdom in private meetings like this. I was always taught if you are the boss you don't need to be the boss. That said, in the field we follow the book, there is only one person in charge, and you are looking at her.

Now then I will tell you all about our "project". The Sapphire Intelligence Unit who you will all have heard of was a total mess, a disgrace, a complete and utter failure. Officers hid and changed evidence, and totally hung victims of rape and sexual abuse out to dry. The victims were not listened to. When they were listened to, they were not believed. When they were believed, it was political to stop listening. This will not happen on my watch.

As a result of their failure, the BSTs have been formed, a simple process rolling Sapphire out into the boroughs. They do a good job but are heavily burdened by administration and procedure. Most importantly their work starts, after the abuse. We start work to stop the abuse. I presume you can see the difference.

In his wisdom and no doubt with an eye on promotion DCS Jonathan Ratcliffe has decided to trial a new team and that's us. We will look to prevent any and all cases of sexual abuse or at least minimise the abuse wherever possible by identifying the toe rags who are carrying it out. Be sure of one thing, if there is just a hint of us making a mistake, or, alternatively, if we are considered to be succeeding at a political cost, Ratcliffe will pull the rug from under our feet, and we will be sent to the basement. Any questions?'

The continuing silence reflected the fact that everyone in the room recognised the seriousness of the situation and anyway the information provided so far would need some filling out before relevant questions could be asked.

'Okay, I'll take that as a no. We will operate alongside patrol units who will identify potential grooming gangs, paedophile rings, possible abuse within families and any other situation where weirdos seek to gratify their disgusting cravings. We will investigate, and in most cases call in task forces to make arrests. We will work closely with the Borough Sapphire Team who will take over once arrests have been made. We will not get any credit for anything we do.'

'Everybody still on board?' The silence was not to Kate's liking. It was due to each individual member of the group digesting a particular point they either hadn't completely understood or were lingering on with interest. 'Sorry I didn't hear you. Am I wasting your time because it seems to me you are certainly wasting mine'?

'Count me in Ma'am I'm right on board.' DS Rashi Kamani was the first to answer followed quickly by his three colleagues. 'So Ma'am will everyone in the building know what we do?'

'They will have an idea. In the early stages I would prefer it if you gave only vague answers to any questions from other officers. They will learn soon enough what we're about. Now let's get to know each other a bit before we get into the nasty stuff. Rashi, you first please.

'Good morning people my name is Rashi Kamani and while I have your attention I would just like to inform you my father owns the best restaurant in town, the Saffron Royale. Don't forget to mention my name for a ten per cent discount. I have been working in 'drugs' and apparently this move will be good for my career. However, from what you have said so far, I think it's more likely to be to do with my heritage than my ability, and will, quite probably, be the end of my career. Still never mind, we are where we are, as my mum says. I am single have a nice apartment downtown and love a good time when I can get out of the restaurant kitchen.'

'Thanks Rashi. Eve would you like to share the reason you are in this motley crew.'

Eve Kendall had been sat, taut, waiting for this moment. She was clearly an attractive woman, but her eyes were cold and even her stylishly cut bobbed blonde hair couldn't soften the innate storm which was so obviously boiling beneath her outward calm.

'I presume you have read my file Ma'am.'

'I have' confirmed Kate.

'Then you will know my answer Ma'am, but you can count me in.'

Kate frowned. 'Fair enough, I respect your privacy for now, but if you want to work with us you will have to open that door slightly at some stage, because everybody here will be depending on you sometime in the future, and they will want to know who that person is that is supposed to have their back.'

Eve stared back at Kate and at each of her new colleagues in turn with a look that dared anyone of them to doubt her.

Without being asked Damian took his turn. 'I live with my mum and little sister Keri. My dad died when I was two and I spent most of my time avoiding trouble on the estate because if I didn't my mum would have killed me. I can tell you she is a damn sight more frightening than any gang leader. As I grew older, I grew bigger and things got easier, helped by my Taekwondo lessons. Mum insisted I took my schooling serious and its totally down to her that I am in the force today. She also makes the best 'jerky' around so don't bother with that Indian rubbish stick to

Jamaican.' DC Damian Lewis smiled broadly at his humour which lasted only as long as Rashi took to remonstrate with him.

'Bangladeshi rubbish, mate.' Rashi hid a grin as he corrected Damian's assertion.

'What?' replied the big man.

'Over eighty per cent of what you would ignorantly call Indian restaurants are owned by Bangladeshis my friend.'

Damian threw an unimpressed look at Rashi while Kate reflected on the fact Damian had not mentioned his work. Was this a sign of a lack of dedication.

'So why do you think you are here Damian.' Kate probed further.

'Probably because I am a large black bloke and somebody has to watch out for you lot, and, like Rashi, I can tick a box for the boss.'

'And what department have you been assigned from?'

'I was on car patrol Ma'am, mostly nights, clubs and pubs, kick out time, plenty of violence a murder here and there. Liked it that way, gave me time to help out at home, you know school runs, bit of cooking, shopping, gave mum a rest like.'

This boy was too good to be true and Kate was feeling he was going to be out of place in the world her team would be working in. She would have to see. 'So that just leaves you DC Campbell.'

Theresa Campbell made a mental note of the fact she was the first one of the team to be referred to using her rank and surname. Nobody else had. 'My friends call me Tess, especially in private meetings like this.' DC Campbell was what other officers might call an "over educated pillock" and more often than not when presented with the opportunity, she inevitably rose to the occasion. 'I have been seconded from CID Ma'am, don't know why. I was happy doing what I was doing, and I was doing it well. The rest of you guys seem to have issues of one type or another but hey, let's see where this takes us.'

The room had become a little less friendly than before as DC

Campbell's words quickly sunk in. Kate Taylor however laughed loudly in an attempt to take the sting out of the situation whilst noticing the obvious thing Tess had clearly missed. 'Yes, let's do that Tess.'

'Now then, let me illustrate to you exactly what you are letting yourselves in for by repeating the words of Baroness Cox in a speech to the 'Lords' in 2019.

"In Rotherham, hundreds of children were sexually exploited between 1997 and 2013. Girls as young as 11 were raped by multiple attackers, trafficked to other towns and cities, and abducted and beaten. Some were doused in petrol and threatened with being set alight, while others were threatened with guns, made to watch brutally violent rapes and warned they would "be next" if they told anyone."

'And there's more. Baroness Cox continued her speech with a case history. She describes how a fifteen year old girl was kidnapped and imprisoned in a house. She said the girl was
"held as a sex slave for 12 years and was repeatedly raped by different members of the grooming gang. She had three forced Sharia marriages, eight forced abortions and two live births. Her abusers referred to her as "white trash". They forced her to wear Islamic dress and permitted her to speak only Urdu and Punjabi."

'That should make you feel sick and incredibly angry, if it doesn't please leave."

Eve was the first to react to the words of the Baroness. 'The people who do this are beneath contempt and I for one am delighted to be given an opportunity to root them out, but do we get a go at the parents as well. What sort of mother or father doesn't see the signs? How can they be so negligent, how do they miss the slow but inevitable decline in the physical and mental wellbeing of their daughters. The total and utter decimation of their kid's life.' The words were uttered with complete scorn and loathing, her previously cold eyes flashed with bitter anger.

'I'm right behind you on that one.' Damian Lewis opened his eyes and ran his hand over his closely shaved head. 'Family is everything, if you can't rely on your people you can't rely on no one.' Kate was pleased that the gentle looking giant was showing a spark. Having spoken however, Damian once more rested his chin on his chest having apparently finished his input on the subject.

'I'm afraid not Eve.' Kate knew from Eve's file she was in dangerous territory here. 'BST deals with the domestics.'

Now are we still all on board. Rashi you've gone quiet. Are you on board?'

'You what!' DS Kamani reacted as if he had just been hit with a baseball bat. 'Ma'am just because I have a beautifully coloured sheen to my skin and I live by the rules of the Qur'an, most of the time, it does not mean I am a throwback to the middle ages. I hope Ma'am that you are not one of those people with deep set prejudices of the type that cause division between the British people, who I might add are both my people and my family's people.'

Kate observed the DS, head tilted, her lip reddening. 'There would appear to be a chip on your shoulder DS Kamani, and you can knock it right off. Actually, I had the impression you weren't listening, so I thought I would wake you up. I think your outburst says a bit more about you than it does about me. Fair comment though and eloquently put. You're on board then?'

'Bloody right Ma'am.' Rashid grinned broadly, a nervous reaction to a sticky situation.

'Rule three broken already. Mend your ways DS Kamani. Any dissenters?' At this point Kate was hoping there weren't, whilst at the same time not being totally convinced by the makeup of her group. They were a long way from where they would need to be. Group cohesion would take time and she was hoping she had it.

'Good everyone safely through round one. Clearly you are all happy with banging up the bullying, soulless reprobates involved in grooming gangs and paedophile rings but are you willing to go further.' Kate let her question float around the room. 'There's no danger to us from the perverts we have been talking about, they are weak, selfish individuals who when caught fold and slink into a corner of self-pity. However, there are others out there with a bit more menace, and I want them as well. I am talking about the east European prostitution rackets and the traffickers both often financed by drug money. If we meet those guys you will need your "A" game.

Kate watched for the reaction this would have on her people, it would be a good exercise for her to understand their character. Eve smiled menacingly, Rashi cupped his chin, slowly stroking his fashionable stubble. Meanwhile Damian showed absolutely no response emotional or physical, while Tess sat unmoved, apparently waiting for what came next. Kate found this interesting, clearly two were relishing the thought of what might almost be considered as an adventure, whereas Lewis and Campbell simply seemed to view the news as a fact of the job, one they would simply get on and do. Either way would do. Kate decided to push the angle.

'Going for these other groups will inevitably lead us into dangerous waters. I am sure you all have firearms training but if I've got that wrong please tell me now.'

The team looked around at each other. 'Don't think Lewis and Kendall will need guns Ma'am their looks should be enough.' Rashi slapped Lewis on the shoulder to emphasise the wisecrack.

Kate looked at the two officers. Sure enough, their faces registered the seriousness they felt for the task ahead. They would be going after hardened criminals, and they would have to rise to the challenge. She had seen enough, it was time to stop the talking, time to start working.

4. Up To Speed

The week had been good for everyone. The team now fully understood the background to their operation, the difficulties they faced, difficulties which had contributed to Sapphires spectacular failure. The pressures it had faced were immense, political, social, emotional, and, for some of the officers involved, the strain on their personal lives had been too great. Clearly the stress had affected judgement at all levels, a few would escape the repercussions, and everyone knew who those "few" would be.

Hundreds of archived cases had been trawled through by Kate's four enthusiastic officers. She certainly could not fault their work ethic or their desire to learn everything they could about the subject that would dominate their lives for the foreseeable future. Most importantly for Kate her colleagues had absorbed the pain and the fear that haunted the "victims". They appreciated the bravery of those who had come forward to expose the voracity of the "grooming gangs" and they acknowledged the despair of those who were still not believed.

Kate had gone out of her way to impress that not all claims of sexual abuse would be true. Fantasists exist and Sapphire's failure to identify these had been a strong force in their downfall. She had repeated the need over and over "innocent until proven guilty", think of the effect on people's lives if they are pursued for a crime they have not committed especially when it involves the abuse of young people.

She held meetings at which she ran through the difficulties in convicting, the unreliability of witnesses, the lack of political will to even discuss certain elements of child abuse and examples of the personal histories and psychology often found in both the abusers and the abused.

Kate had emphasised the need for her team to be physically fit. She made them undergo, self-defence training, practiced restraint and control methods, and as all four officers had passed their firearms training, target practice. All of this helped to break up the monotony of desk work and helped the team gel through competitive motivation. Individuals were developing nicely, the team, was still flawed.

The week seemed to fly by, and the moment of truth was dawning, but not before the weekend had been enjoyed and a meeting with DCS Ratcliffe had been endured. 'Okay everybody.' It was time to wrap up. Kate had submitted her initial report and the time was drawing near when the team's private lives would go very much on hold. 'First thank you for your work, this week has been a hard trawl, but it was very necessary because if you are not prepared, if you do not have the knowledge, your skills will be of no use. If you do not understand the depth of depravity, the darkness, the loss of all hope that is out there you will not cope. You will have seen why those who went before failed. You will understand the "forces" that oppose our work, you will appreciate the job that needs to be done. Knowing all of this, are you still with me?'

Something had changed in the people who now stared at Kate. These were not the same four officers who had started the week. Five days ago each of them had been going along doing a good job, in a routine, aware of the dangers every police officer faces on an almost daily basis, but none of them had ever expected to be involved in a task force of such intensity. Five days ago, she had asked if everyone was "on board" and she had received a stuttering response which gave her no confidence moving forward, today she received an animal roar of approval.

'That confirmation was inspiring, thank you.' Kate clapped her team enthusiastically, not something she would normally do, she found such actions patronising and cliched, but today her reaction was instinctive, it meant something, and she beamed with pride. 'I would like to invite you to join me for a swift half in the Railway in twenty minutes, drinks are on me and then you can get on with your weekend. Pack in as much as you can because as from Monday we belong to "every mothers' daughter". If you can't make it to the pub don't worry, see you Monday.'

Kate was slightly disappointed but not surprised. She prided herself on her analysis of character and in this she had not been let down. Rashi and Tess sat at the table with her, the former a glass of bottled non-alcoholic beer in front of him. Tess held a small pinot, looking longingly but not yet sipping. A team, as yet did not exist.

'I reckon the three of us have earned this.' Kate opened the conversation and raised her half of shandy. 'To success.'

Rashi and Tess followed suit before the inevitable, short embarrassing silence ensued. 'So, what can you tell us boss?' Rashi as usual was first in. He wasn't sure why he had asked the question and was not surprised at the answer.

'Sorry Rashi, no offence but we haven't reached full trust levels just yet and that works both ways. I can tell you you've all been brilliant this week and I am confident I will come away from my meeting with DCS Ratcliffe on Monday with the green light.'

Kate switched the stage to Tess who had worked diligently and cleverly during the week finding one of the gems hidden in the patrol reports. 'Any plans for the weekend Tess?'

'No, not really.' That seemed to have been the girl's response to almost any enquiry made of her by any of her colleagues over the last few days. 'Are Muslims allowed to drink alcohol Rashi?' Tess had deflected the attention to her DS and Kate "filed" her use of that particular technique for later use.

'In Bangladesh we might say, "You drink alcohol! It's haram; you filthy spoiled rich!" Rough translation.'

'But what does the Qur'an actually teach.'

'Alcohol comes under the heading of "forbidden", although as with any religion there is debate. The Qur'an for example really only states that "wine" is forbidden, or at least that is one interpretation that could be used to justify drinking a few beers.'

'And do you use that justification Rashi?' Tess certainly didn't let go even when she probably should. Rashi, however, seemed quite happy to instruct his interrogator in the mysteries of his religion. He knew he was rather light on the subject, but he also knew he had enough in his head to deal with any flippant questions he inevitably had thrown at him. He was calm he wouldn't be baited.

'If I were living in Bangladesh, I would probably not drink any alcohol, both because I would not wish to do so, but also because there are harsh punishments if you do. But me, I am a British boy, I take my religion seriously, but I doubt there is a religion on this earth whose followers comply fully with all of its tenets. In short, I don't completely avoid alcohol, but I do avoid excessive use of it. Do you have a religion Tess?'

'My mum is Indian, and my dad is a white Yorkshireman. In case you hadn't noticed I am a half caste luckily I have managed to slip between the grubby fingers of religion.'

Kate was surprised by the sudden aggression in Tess's voice. She welcomed it but changed the subject. 'Tell me Tess before you became embroiled with us lot what were your career plans. You quite clearly had your path mapped out in your head.'

'To go as far as I can go Ma'am.'

Pulling teeth was probably easier but Kate could be insistent too. 'And how far did you envisage that being Tess?'

Tess felt the slight aggravation in her boss' tone and decided that just this once she would offer a little more insight into her ambitions, but not her life, that was personal, it needed to be protected. Her dad had told her *"don't open up with any of them, mark my words they will use it against you when the time suits them. Keep your head down and keep climbing"*. She thought for a while longer before answering. 'I would really like to become a top murder detective. And what about you Ma'am where do you want to go?'

Kate shook her head, sucked her lower lip, and breathed slowly out through her nose. Tess had done it again, a few words and move on. 'I am where I want to be, now we have to perform on the big stage. The bad news Tess is we all climb or fall together on this one, but make an impression alongside your colleagues, and it will certainly help you to get a good hand up the ladder.'

Tess let the words sink in, mulled them over and came to a conclusion she wasn't about to share. 'Thank you for the drink Ma'am but I must go, I've arranged to meet a few of the girls for a drink and a Chinese. See you both Monday.'

Rashi and Kate watched Tess disappear through the pub door neither of them willing to make comment. 'Me too Ma'am, I promised to help dad out in the kitchen tonight, my good deed for the weekend so that the rest of the time is "my time". After this week I think I need it.'

Kate smiled. 'I think we all do. Enjoy yourself Rashi, make the most of it.'

Rashi too, exited out into a night already darkening, a cold breeze sneaking through the door as it slowly closed behind him. Kate scratched her head before ordering a small whiskey and coke.

Rashi arrived at the Saffron Royale long before Kate left the Railway and as usual was met with an embrace from his adoring mum.

'Such a boy, your grandfather would be proud, a police officer, our own batman.'

'Loxborough is hardly Gotham City mum.' Rashi had been a "police officer" for nearly fifteen years now and still he had to go through this regular ritual. He was more than happy to do so. His parents had wanted him to be a lawyer or a doctor maybe an engineer, but he wasn't, and they still managed to bathe in his position of relative authority.

'Let me be a mother Rashi, let me bathe in pleasure at my son's success.' Rashi placed his arm warmly around his mother's slender shoulders welcoming the comfort he always felt when he was with her. 'It's dad who is the hero, never stops working, never stops giving. In my eyes he is a legend and together you are my world. Now where's my apron?'

Aanshi pulled him tighter. Her name meant "God's gift" but for her there was only one gift from God in the house, and that was Rashi.

5. Home From Home

Eve strolled out of the drizzle into the warmth and banter of the Kings Arms, her home from home. She had enjoyed a lazy day and was in the mood for a good night out. Her small terraced house was only ninety metres or so away, but she preferred the "ambience" of the pub to the unlived in blandness of her "home". Before leaving for the "Kings" she had contemplated yet again making some changes to her property, maybe a bit of paint, new tiles in the bathroom, a bigger kitchen and, maybe not. The room she saw most of was her bedroom. She had that just the way she liked it, brilliantly retro 60s, red, white and black, plenty of politically incorrect plastic. She grinned at the thought.

'Something tickled you has it Eve? Same as usual?' Harry Allerton was a "class" landlord. Not in the cultural sense just in the "How to run a pub sense". He looked the picture, overweight, shining bald head, large veined nose and laughing eyes. He also packed a punch as many an overzealous local had discovered. His pub was his life, his regulars his family.

'Just thinking about decorating my house Harry but I decided I would probably make it look worse than it already is with my sense of décor.' Eve loved the pub and she adored the people who frequented it. She grew up in the area and would likely never leave. They all knew she was a cop but they also all knew she was at heart "one of them". They were her people, high in traditional morals, protective of their own, and quick to hand out retribution to those who failed their sense of decency and "proper" standards. On top of that they were great fun.

'So, fancy your chances in the quarters tonight do we Eve?' "Chancer" Evans had arrived at the bar. 'Pint of lager please Harry.'

'Against "Pinky"? What do you think?' Eve looked at him enquiringly, head tilted to one side, one eyebrow raised. It was the last eight of the pub pool competition and her defeat in the semis last year still rankled.

'Oh you'll beat Pinky all right, but don't fancy you in the semis, reckon you'll bottle it again.' Chancer was living up to his name but luckily for him Eve was well up for pub banter.

'Fancy a little flutter then do we Evans? How about twenty quid I make it to the final.' Eve knew her adversary and he certainly didn't have the manhood to take a bet of that size. Chancer choked over giving fifty pence to Comic Relief, he would now be having kittens at the thought of losing twenty smackers.

'Only kidding Eve my money is on you to win it girl.' The wiry, slightly crouched figure disappeared as quickly as he had arrived and Eve sipped her pint, smiling mischievously to herself.

Punters continued to file into the pub, the majority of them stopping to have a word with Eve, however small. Some simply touched her shoulder in acknowledgement, one or two gave her a peck on the cheek, nobody touched her hair. But one man with broad shoulders and hard features stayed longer. Kate had known him since she was a child, he had a reputation of sorts, both good and bad depending on who you spoke to. Either way he was grudgingly respected. There was always one in every pub community.

'Eve I hear there's a fellow living in Redlake, just been let out of prison, child offender. Word is he's not welcome if you know what I mean. Knowing your background, I thought you might be interested.' This man, Jack Crawford, wasn't referring to Eve's professional life, he didn't yet know about her new position and what it involved.

'What do you think I can do about it Jack?'

'Have a word in the right ears, get him moved for his own safety. Listen Eve, Redlake's not my manor I'm just giving you some gossip, make of it what you will, but do you remember Terry Frost, played darts for the Plough, bit loud, apparently can be a bit punchy.'

Eve cast her mind back a few weeks to the game between the Kings and the boys from Redlake. 'Yes, a bit loud after a few pints but he seemed cheery enough though.'

'Well he's got a thing about paedos. Just saying Eve. Good luck tonight, I'll see you in the final girl.'

Eve reflected on just how strange life could be. One week into the job and she was getting unsolicited leads, mind you in her part of town she was the "go to" for anything the locals were uneasy about. They usually gave her some breathing space to do "things the right way" before it was sorted out the "old way".

It was just after nine o'clock when Eve's quarter final was called to the pool table. She or Pinky would be the last of the four semi-finalists decided tonight. Jack Crawford, Laura Tenby and Kev Laine had already won their matches and quite a large number of drinkers were now showing an interest in the final nine games about to be played.

'Won't be needing more than five games tonight', declared Pinky confidently, before proceeding to miss the rack completely.

'You're right about that,' replied Eve as she smacked the cue ball against the tip of the triangle and saw the first ball of the night drop into a corner pocket. This set the pattern for the rest of the match although Eve required seven games to see off an extremely poor challenger.

With a couple of hours left before closing, the music was

turned up, resulting in the level of conversation also ratcheting up a couple of notches. Harry and his barmaid Jennie were being kept on their toes, but it didn't stop the girl from taking part in snatched conversations with Eve and Laura Tenby who was always a good laugh. When the time came to leave, Harry passed a small carrier bag over the bar to Eve. 'There's a nice little curry in their darling, help soak up the wet stuff.'

Eve kissed Harry on the top of his bald head which he had offered in the customary way, a silly little tradition they had followed for as long as they could remember. Why they did it was beyond them. Sliding from her chair Eve blew a kiss to Jennie, hugged Laura and made for the door.

'See you tomorrow for the footie, Eve?'

'Wouldn't miss it for the world Harry. Up the Toon.'

'Really don't know why a Sheffield girl supports that lot,' shouted Laura.

'Alan Shearer, Kevin Keegan, 1990s, what's not to love. See you guys.' Eve turned, staggered slightly, and walked out into a cold damp night with Saturday's dinner held tightly in her hand. 'Bliss' she muttered to herself 'Absolute Bliss.'

6. Family Matters

Tracy finished her drawing, a bright red apple, small green leaf, and short black stalk, beside it a penguin. She passed it to her dad. 'Look daddy.'

Her father leaned forward putting down his newspaper eagerly taking the girl's work from her outstretched hand. 'Wow that's so good darling, is there a story behind it, is the penguin hungry?'

'No' replied the little girl. 'I just wanted to draw an apple and then I wanted to draw a penguin.'

Her father looked at her adoringly. 'Come and look at this mum, Tracy's a proper little artist. A slim woman entered the room removing her apron as she walked. She flicked several strands of her jet black hair from her eyes and bent down placing a loving arm around her daughter's shoulders.

'Let's see now. That's fantastic angel you're being such a good girl while mummy makes the dinner.' Tracy smiled contentedly snuggling into the warmth of her mother's arms.

'Can I help you with the dinner now mummy?'

'Of course you can poppet. I'm just about to make an apple crumble so you can help me make the crumbs.' Mother and daughter moved into the kitchen of the open plan house and began collecting the ingredients of the pudding together. A large bowl stood waiting to accept their playful fingers.

Tracy's dad sat back in his chair raising his paper to read. He lowered it just for a moment breathing in the sight of the two girls in his life. He nodded to himself and turned once more to the sports pages. There could be no doubt in anyone's mind, Terry Frost was devoted to his family.

A short while later Tracy peered round the door to the lounge, a smudge of flour graced her nose, butter stuck to her fingers. 'We are going to the swimming pool tomorrow aren't we dad?' She rubbed a clot of crumbs from the wall hoping she wouldn't be seen whilst creating a bigger mess.

Terry laughed. 'If you ask me again I'll go bonkers you little monkey. Yes we are going for a swim, yes I am going to teach you to swim a bit further, yes we will have a warm drink from the machine, and yes, we will stop and buy an ice cream on the way home. Is that okay young lady?'

'Think that just about covers it.'

Tracy's head disappeared once more and left her dad to contemplate how lucky he was to have such a beautiful family.

The phone was ringing. Why was the phone ringing on a Sunday? Eve grabbed her phone. 'Ten sodding twenty on a Sunday and my phone is ringing.' Eve hesitated not recognising the number before pressing the green button.

'Hello.'

'Hi Eve, it's Jack Crawford.'

'Why?' Eve was struggling to focus and eager to end the conversation before it started.

'Sorry to disturb you love but do you remember what I was saying last night about Redlake and Terry Frost?'

'Sort of.'

'It's kicked off down at the Community centre, Frosty is in

trouble and he's not good with his temper if you know what I mean.'

'So, what's it got to do with me Jack?' Eve knew exactly what it had to do with her, and she recognised a favour being called in when she heard it. Before Jack could reply Eve already rising from her bed confirmed acceptance of the request. 'On my way Jack.'

By the time Eve arrived at the community centre two patrol cars were parked outside and a group of bystanders had already formed by the entrance. Two constables stood guard. Eve stepped toward them and proffered identification. 'Where's the action and what happened' she demanded.

'Pool area Ma'am. A man's been assaulted, the assailant claims the guy "touched" his daughter.' Eve felt her anger rising, loosened her shoulders, swept by, and made for the pool. Inside she found Terry Frost backed up and swearing at three constables who were doing their best to calm him down. Sitting, nose bleeding, eyes dazed, sat a plump man of middle age a look of indignation on his face.

Eve ignored him and instead marched up to the figure surrounded by police officers. 'Terry Frost isn't it?'

The dark haired bull like man glared at her before recognition dawned and he relaxed his taut muscles, the veins on his head popping less violently.

'So, what happened Mr Frost?' Eve adopted her stern, "I'm listening" voice.

Although Terry Frost had calmed down on seeing Eve, having to excuse his actions, which he considered to be more than justified, and, to his mind sparingly executed, saw his temperature rise again. 'That git touched my daughter, he's lucky I didn't kill him'

'I think you will find you are the one who is lucky there was no killing. I'm afraid you can't just take the law into your own hands Mr Frost.' Eve turned to the constables. 'Take the other chap down to the station and take his statement, if he has one to make. I'll follow you down with this one. One of you wait outside to accompany me.' Eve was feeling tetchy and others were getting the fall out.

Two of the officers helped the older looking man to his feet. Despite his discomfort both from the bloody nose and the accusations, he was clearly regaining his composure and stressing his innocence, whilst exaggerating the violence of his alleged attacker as he left the hall with his escort.

'Should have left it to us Terry, at worse make a civilian arrest, something a bit more restrained perhaps?'

'Wouldn't know how to make one of those and anyway, what would you have done if a bloody paedo touched your kid?'

Eve knew the answer but they both knew she couldn't express it. Her head was starting to throb, this was not how Sunday mornings were supposed to be spent. Footie was on soon and now Terry bloody Frost had created a pile of paperwork. If she missed the first half she was not going to be happy.

'You need to come with me to the station Terry. I'll get someone to take your statement and then you can go home but you will end up in court if the man you allegedly hit insists on taking action against you. If what you say is true, then I doubt it is in his interest to do so. But please Terry don't do it again, stay away, leave this to us. Where's your daughter?'

'I sent her home with the wife.'

'And how are they both?' Eve refrained from making a comment about his description of the girl's mother, it was a phrase she didn't much like but now was not the time.

'The missus is spitting feathers, but I don't think my daughter really knows what the fuss is all about she just knows that pervert touched her bum.'

'Ok, Perfect. Come on, Let's get this over and done with.'

Eve sat with the station Sergeant as the paperwork was duly

transcribed. 'What shall I do with him now Ma'am?'

'As far as I am aware there haven't been any charges yet so send him home Sarge.'

Before leaving the station, DS Kendall sought out the constable who had ridden to the station with her and requested a lift back to her car at the Community Centre. The young officer was happy to oblige, and Eve took the opportunity to make a "friend" who might just be useful in the future.

Eve arrived fifteen minutes late for the game. 'Usual Eve?' Jennie Hargreaves was always on duty for the football matches. Eve loved just being able to talk girly stuff with someone who didn't even know the meaning of the word "malice" let alone practise it. Are you recovering from a night out love 'cos you look cream crackered.'

Jenny's words amused Eve. Cockney rhyming slang just didn't sound right when it was delivered in a strong Yorkshire accent. 'I've had a long day already Jennie, still the good news is it can't get any worse for a Sunday.'

'I'm afraid you spoke to soon Eve, the "Toon" are already two goals down.'

'Bollocks' muttered Eve and downed her pint in one.

7. When The Scarecrow Doesn't Move

'Come in DI Taylor, close the door and sit down.' Chief Detective Superintendent Ratcliffe spoke crisply as if eager to get things off his mind. His hair was ruffled, only slightly, and his tie was not tight to his neck. Anyone who knew Ratcliffe would consider this unusual.

'You have had a week now to get your team settled down and I have received your first full report for which I thank you.'

There was a "however" coming, of that there was no doubt. Kate was unperturbed as she was prepared for some form of put down. In fact, she was prepared for an ongoing stream of put downs for the foreseeable future.

'I see you have sifted out a number of reports of possible grooming gang activity in several different parts of the area. Why do you think these patrol reports weren't followed up DI Taylor?'

This had been an easy one to forecast and Kate gave a confident reply. 'Insufficient evidence and unreliable witnesses Sir.'

'And why are these witnesses considered to be unreliable.'

'Unfortunately, most of the witnesses will have been plied with alcohol and drugs to such an extent their versions of events cannot be relied on in a court of law. This is because their statements can be vague, often self-contradictory, their descriptions of events changing over time. They find it difficult to explain events in fine detail and have an inability or reluctance to describe the "perpetrator", Sir.'

'Good Kate, you have been doing your homework. So why do you think you can do anything with them when all those who have come before you haven't?'

Kate accepted her boss's patronising comment with the disdain it deserved. 'There is only insufficient evidence because nobody has tried to find any Sir. Let me look for it and then we can compile some solid witness reports to go with it, Sir.'

The Superintendent could tell Kate Taylor was chomping at the bit, but in his mind, that, whilst being commendable, was also dangerous. A loose cannon was the last thing he needed.

'Of the seven or eight cases you have identified as worthy of your team's attention I feel comfortable with two. These are identified in your report as cases one and five.'

Kate clenched her fists below the desk in celebration. She wanted to shout out in acknowledgment of her achievement. Her negotiation skills had shown their worth, ask for eight items settle for two. Just make sure they are the two you want.

'Di Taylor you must be aware there is a political angle to our work. Certain politicians go out of their way to create racial tensions by declaring our work as racist. We can't change the statistics, we both know grooming gangs are made up of men who are eighty five per cent Pakistani. This fact is repeatedly 'covered up' by certain journalists of a particular political slant who claim we have an agenda against Muslims. They can destroy careers. Please bear this in mind not just for now but for the future.'

'Sir, perhaps somebody can tell me what is remotely Islamic about alcohol, drugs and abusing daughters. The people involved in these grooming gangs are predators, pure and simple.'

'You are right of course Kate.' Ratcliffe wanted this meeting to end. 'You can pay some attention to the two cases we have discussed, but DI Taylor'. Ratcliffe paused unsure whether to trust

Kate with what he was about to say. 'Find some new cases, and for goodness sake Kate, please find some with white men involved.

'Settle down. You've had a week of lazing around the office, it's now time to get busy. No doubt you want to know how the meeting went with his lordship. It's good news. He's allowing us to follow up the two cases we all felt we wanted to crack. First one is the one you found Tess. Let me remind you all about that incident. If you remember, a night patrol reported a girl had approached the officers who were sat in their car close to a kebab shop in St Annes Road, Roche. They were there as a result of neighbours complaining about the noise they had to put up with at night from the takeaway's customers. The girl who they estimated to be about fourteen told them she was being abused and that she had been "asked to recruit other teenagers". She told the constables that her abusers "specified that they wanted only white girls". The Patrol report stated the girl was clearly on drugs and smelt strongly of alcohol.'

Kate sifted through the paperwork in her hands. 'They said she had become "tense and aggressive", before moving quickly away. No action was taken. Apparently patrols get this all the time. Have you experienced anything like this on night watch DC Lewis?'

'No Ma'am, well yes Ma'am, I mean not young girls saying they have been abused, but certainly plenty of abuse from women who have had one too many. Worse than the men they are. So vicious.' Damian shook his head at the thought. 'All they want to do is fight you or lick you. At least the men, normally keep to making what they think are funny comments about the police. Until the women "egg" them on that is. I remember...'

'Have you finished Lewis?' Kate waited for a few moments to confirm Lewis had stopped talking. 'Good.'

'Sorry Ma'am.' Kate's lip received its first punishment of the day.

Kate had spoken to the officers who had written the report almost as soon as Tess had unearthed it. She had been confident Ratcliffe would allow her at least one case to pursue and even if he hadn't, this one was always going to be investigated by her team, no matter what. She had discovered there had been numerous complaints about the takeaway with vehicles continuously drawing up and men clogging the streets. There had also been reports of young girls hanging around getting drunk and shouting at the neighbours. Kate knew this was a mixed bag, but she had to get to the bottom of it, one way or another.

'This is going to be a difficult first case guys. We have nothing concrete and quite frankly the reports we do have about the area and its "goings on" are from neighbours annoyed at the disturbance to their sleep. We have had nothing from them to suggest grooming gangs, but, I think we all have a small itch about this one that needs scratching. 'DC Lewis, DS Kamani you're on stake out tonight.'

'Why us Ma'am?' Rashi's question was delivered with a tone that made the point he was making, too obvious.

Kate viewed him through narrowing eyes and could not avoid the conclusion that a not too subtle version of both barrels was required

'In case you hadn't realised this is a covert action. We are attempting to make ourselves inconspicuous. You DS Kamani are of Asian descent, and Lewis, as you may have observed is black. Let that sink in and then ask me another stupid question. No don't bother, you and Lewis take the night off and I will stick two attractive white police officers in a car opposite the site of a potential grooming gang's operations. I am sure they will not be noticed or maybe I am wrong DS Kamani.'

'Apologies Ma'am.' Rashi knew he had a small chip on his

shoulder, normally he tried to keep it low key, unfortunately he too frequently let it mould his thinking.

'You are of course absolutely right Ma'am and me and Lewis are the best officers for the stake out.'

Kate however was not prepared to let it go there. 'And why are you the best officers for the job DS Kamani?'

'Because I am Bangladeshi, and Lewis is black Ma'am.'

'DS Kamani you are wrong again. Is this a flaw in your character? Do you make a habit of making mistakes because if you do please notify the team, immediately.'

Rashi was up to his neck in it and still digging. It had to stop but Kate Taylor's last outburst had him stumped.

'Listen and listen good.' Kate was in no mood for any hint of racial undertones in her team. To her every one of them was a police officer fighting injustice and downright evil, her team had to be "brothers in arms". 'What you should have said is you are a British police officer, the son of a hardworking, decent, loving family and that DC Lewis, is exactly the same. You should then have observed that due to the heritage apparent in the visages of yourself and Lewis you will be the two members of our new team who can best perform the task presented to us. You might then have added that DS Kendall and DC Campbell will perform the task when we embark on our campaign against white paedophiles and that when we turn our attention to east European prostitution rackets and Chinese slavers we will probably mix things up a bit.'

Kate paused for effect. 'And what will we do to all of the above DS Kendall'.

Eve smiled gently and rose from her seat for added effect. 'Crush the bastards Ma'am.'

Tess Campbell who up to now had taken no part in proceedings took the opportunity to move the meeting on. 'So, what will DS Kendall and me be doing Ma'am.'

Kate Taylor was glad of the intervention and the opportunity to progress.

'You DC Campbell will, alongside DS Kendall, be canvassing the area. I want you to talk to shopkeepers, landlords and locals on the pretext of carrying out a survey of crime in general. I want you to tell the community we have had reports of burglaries, drunkenness, drugs and prostitution in the area. Let's see what information this provides. Ask them if there is anyone they don't trust, do they feel comfortable in taxis, do they feel safe at night. Let's see what comes out of the woodwork. Now's as good a time as any to get started so here are some forms I've had drawn up for you to make notes on. I'll catch up with you later shall we say Gino's on Bennett Street at sixteen hundred hours?'

'That's fine Ma'am. Come on Tess let's have a chat and then we can get going. See you later guys.' Eve led Tess to a couple of desks in the corner and sat down to discuss their day's movements and aims.

Kate turned to her two male colleagues. 'You two get yourself off for a couple of hours, you've got a long shift ahead tonight and probably for the rest of the week. Please start your night at nineteen hundred hours. While you are on surveillance duty you will not intervene in any minor crimes you may witness. Unless its murder or rape call the situation in and make notes for our records. It is vital your presence is not noted so don't stay in one place too long unless you are certain you are undetectable. Drive around the area a few times to break the monotony, but if you do keep your eyes open for anything which could be remotely connected to grooming. Have you got that? Any questions? Please come in tomorrow around ten thirty when we can have a debrief on today's activities. If you need me tonight for whatever reason call me. You both have my number, right?'

'Yes Ma'am.' Rashi acknowledged Kates instructions while Damian searched his phone contacts, appearing to be having problems finding Kate's number. She waited for a frustrating length of time.

'Problem DC Lewis?'

'Can't remember what I put you under Ma'am. It's not DI or Taylor and it's not Kate or boss.'

'Well it's going to be very interesting when we find out how exactly you have logged me isn't it Lewis.'

'It's okay I've got it Ma'am.' There was huge relief on his face. He had not been relishing the attention.

'And where was it logged?' Kate was trying desperately hard to hide a smile whilst maintaining an air of unimpressed authority.

'Under Ma'am, Ma'am. Think I'd better change that, or I might get confused with Mum, Ma'am.'

'Whatever Lewis, now both of you get off home. I will check in with you sometime during the night. Good luck and good hunting.'

Kate moved over to see if Tess and Eve required anything of her before wishing them well and leaving the room to visit 'control'. It was important they knew about the surveillance patrol and not to attempt to contact them, whilst at the same time accepting any calls for support or for reports of minor crimes from them. In all probability nothing would take place tonight but if it did, she and her team would be ready, make no mistake.

8. The Modern Office

Gino's was a neat, slightly old fashioned café, the type that has an ingrained ambience built up over the years, warm, clean, comforting. The owner always smiled while his wife never stopped cooking, cleaning and fussing over her clientele. Every time you visited you were asked to try a new cake that had been baked that morning, or a small slice of a tart not before seen on the menu.

On top of the bonhomie and delicious freebees the coffee was just perfect. Kate reminisced about how difficult it had been to find the right bitter sweet combination, Starbucks, Costa Coffee, Number One, forget it, Gino's every time.

She was looking forward to catching up with the two female members of her team. She liked to cover all angles and a feminine view of the project would be interesting to put alongside the thoughts of Lewis and Kamani at some point. More importantly she was desperate for some feedback on their first case.

Eve and Tess arrived some twenty minutes late. Another time this would have resulted in a short swift wrap on the knuckles, but Kate knew that canvassing was a back breaker and the two officers did not deserve a reprimand for sticking to the job.

'By the looks on your faces you've had a long day and by the look of your folders you've had a productive day.'

Before Kate could get an answer, Daniela loomed. Gino's wife had beautiful thick deep jet hair and a wonderful motherly face, big eyes, plump lips, and a fine Italian nose. She placed a plate of half a dozen fingers of what looked like cherry tart on the table. 'Eat girls and tell me what you think, be honest now while I fetch your drinks. Two coffees? And another for you Katie?'

Eve and Tess nodded in reply, Kate declined the offer. They looked at each other and smiled contentedly. 'As far as I am concerned those tarts are great, fantastic and I won't let anyone say anything different' Eve made her comment with a fearful expression on her face. 'I once made the mistake of saying one of her cupcakes had too much sugar, and boy, did I get some grief. Won't make that mistake again.'

Tess laughed while Kate remembered a similar experience with some ginger biscuits. 'So tell me, how has your afternoon been.'

Eve opened her folder. 'I suggest we answer that question individually, that way we might get a good subjective feel for what we have found on the doorstep and then we can look at the detail for a more objective view. Tess you go first.'

Tess reached for her file, but Eve stopped her. 'Just from memory Tess, give us an impression. It's a good training exercise, more often than not what we think we have seen and heard is not what the facts tell us later.'

'Okay.' Daniela reappeared with the coffees. 'There ladies' She looked nosily at the files on the table. 'What are you talking about today? Anything interesting?'

'We are just doing a bit of research Daniela, making sure the neighbourhoods safe.' Kate wanted to get on with the meeting, but she didn't want to appear rude. 'Do you feel safe Daniela?'

'Safe? Of course I am safe. I have lived here for over twenty years and I can tell you it is a lovely place to be. We are very happy, and we have such lovely neighbours, so peaceful, so nice.'

'Thank you for that.' Kate smiled and then deliberately

turned her attention to her colleagues. Daniela could not miss the meaning of Kate's gesture and slid slowly back to her husband behind the counter where she no doubt made some comment about being snubbed.

Tess breathed in, turned her eyes to the window and back to the table. 'I have to say that what I have heard today is pretty much tittle tattle. Typical neighbours' complaints about the young making too much noise, too many cars going up and down, the need for more buses and corner shops. However, there were also some moans about drug users waiting for drop offs and rough looking individuals. Most of the neighbours appear to have decided they are "Romanians". I guess in reality they could be any eastern European sounding blokes.

'That is interesting Tess.' said Kate. 'What about you then Eve.

'You're right it is interesting because my experience was the same and it is the last bit that bothers me. Let's be honest we are here looking for grooming gangs. Statistics say they are most likely to be Asian and here we are receiving complaints about white "Romanians." And what is just as intriguing is neither of us have mentioned any suggestion of potential abuse victims. Something isn't adding up.'

Kate agreed. 'Can we put some figures on this.'

'Yes, we drew up a form to enable us to break down into categories the things we were being told. We used six headings, Violent disturbance, burglary, Potential abuse, unsafe areas, drugs and "other" under which we put the general day to day complaints, and we spent ten minutes compiling the results before we came over to meet you. Tess and Eve opened their files. 'Go on Tess you do the honours.'

Tess looked incredibly pleased to have centre stage again and having briefly swept her eyes over the paperwork she addressed the findings. 'I'll start with burglaries. Apparently, there were a spate of them at the beginning of the year, but several arrests have pretty much resulted in an end to them. The overall feeling is that this is a safe area although there is no obvious desire to be out late at night. Noise and the occasional outburst of violence is for the most part blamed on people passing through. However, these occurrences seem to be most prevalent to the east of the patch we covered, with the crossover into Parklands Estate. Similarly, that seems to be where the drug activity is centred with reports of small groups of people waiting for drop offs. The residents were quick to point out that these incidents had been reported to the police by them, but nothing had been done. Neither of us picked up any sense of girls being abused, but there were a couple of suggestions of prostitutes appearing, again this was in the east. The "others" we've covered.

'Thanks' Tess, that was well summarised. Eve what do you make of it?'

'I suggest Tess and I spend more time over in Parklands tomorrow boss, get a better idea of the lay of the land, followed perhaps by an evening sortie.'

'Makes sense Eve. Right thanks for a good day's work. I'm going to liaise with the lads later and we will meet up in the morning to put all the feedback together. Have a good evening, well done.' Kate went to the till and settled up not forgetting to heap the requisite amount of praise on Daniela for her amazing tarts. This actually took longer than she had hoped and by the time she had finished, Eve and Tess had already gone.

DS Kamani and DC Lewis had spent a dull two hours in a warm but uncomfortable unmarked vehicle. Damian was totally used to night patrols but with the ones he was used to you actually moved around a bit. Tonight, they were sat in one place, viewing in perpetuity, one scene. At least it was fairly vibrant. It was amazing how many people accepted the challenge of eating a kebab with its fat oozing down and through the pitta bread, it's final resting place the arteries of the blissfully happy consumer.

Lewis offered his partner a brown bag stuffed with Caribbean patties first removing one for himself, greedily stuffing it into his welcoming mouth. His pleasure was evident on his satisfied face.

'Bloody Hell Damian how much more food have you brought with you? We've had spicy chicken wings and cheesy sausages and now your mum's version of a small Cornish pasty, how many more courses have you got stashed away in your bag?'

'You learn to be prepared when you've done a few patrols, it makes the time go quicker if you have a few things to eat and a cuppa or two to wash it down. If you're complaining, I'll eat the rest myself.'

Rashi smiled. 'No mate they're great. Respect to your mum.'

At that moment the phone rang. 'Ma'am's calling in.' DI Kamani answered the call putting it on loudspeaker for Damian to listen in.

'Evening DS Kamani have you anything of interest for me?'

Rashi took a deep breath. 'To be honest Ma'am it's a typical night outside any normal kebab shop. Comings and goings lots of laughter, people milling around waiting outside, taxis drawing up on a regular basis, mainly it seems for takeaway deliveries.'

'Any groups of young people?'

'Yes Ma'am, threes and fours, mixed gender, mixed race Ma'am. Groups of young people having fun. Nothing suspicious.'

'Okay thanks DS Kamani. Your colleagues have had some interesting chats with the neighbours, and I suggest you hang around for another hour or so. Come in for a debrief meeting tomorrow morning when we can pool our initial thoughts and findings and move on from there.'

'Fair enough Ma'am. See you tomorrow.' Rashi turned to DC Lewis. 'That's a result. I thought she'd keep us out here all night leaving me at the mercy of the contents of your holdall.'

'There's always tomorrow,' replied Damian with a wicked grin on his face, and once my mum knows how much you enjoyed her cuisine, those bags of goodies are just going to multiply.'

Rashi let out a loud exaggerated groan. 'I'll take the time to stock up with a few more Rennies then mate. Goodness knows how I'm going to sleep with all this heavy stuff lining my stomach.'

9. Never A Lull

Kate had unexpectedly, slept well. The team had begun their mission after what seemed a long, dour period of training and research. She now sat wating for her colleagues to arrive for the update on the first day's progress. She already knew the main themes of the previous day's canvassing and stake out. The only thing that had really come out of it all were questions relating to the eastern side of the area, more likely to be relating to drugs, than grooming gangs. Her team would have to investigate and then more likely than not hand over to the Drugs Squad. Still better a result than no result at all.

Rashi as always arrived first. 'Morning Ma'am.'

'How are you this morning?' Kate asked the question but it was nothing more than a throwaway line, one of those questions you ask, but couldn't care less what the answer is.

'Stomach took a bit of a pasting last night Ma'am, DC Lewis came stocked with goodies for the night. Actually the food was great but don't tell him or we won't be able to get in the car later for holdalls full of Jamaican Specials.'

Their banter was interrupted by the arrival of DS Kendall, DC Campbell and swiftly on their tails, DC Lewis.

'Okay guys let's get straight into this.' Before Kate could progress any further there was a knock on the door, and a smartly cropped head poked itself inside.

'Sorry to disturb you Kate.' She hated apologies. In her experience they usually weren't meant. 'But we have a situation and the Chief is demanding everyone respond including you guys. You're all needed at briefing room four.' DI Trent Kruse looked flushed, clearly operating on adrenaline, his normal calm exterior and laid-back attitude badly ruffled.

Kate had for an instant been annoyed by the intrusion but seeing DI Kruse was in no mood to be baulked, or kept waiting, she barked a short command. 'Everybody up.' Trent Kruse had already disappeared and within seconds Kate and her team were not far behind him.

Ratcliffe was already in the meeting room waiting for the remaining officers to join him. 'That'll have to do. Anybody arriving late can pick up the pieces from their colleagues. We have a hostage situation at a robbery gone wrong in the high street Those of you who are in this room are the only available units. It's not proper but weapons are on the table for all trained firearms officers. Check them, sign the form and I will sort the paperwork and any comeback. DI Taylor you are to take operational control on site. Get down there now, assess and report.' There was a silence which lasted no more than a couple of seconds as minds switched into procedural mode but even this was too long for Ratcliffe. 'What are you bloody wating for, get out.' Go!'

All seven officers raced to the car park, Kate talking animatedly to Trent Kruse on the way. 'We are likely to be arriving late in the action so go straight to the rear of the property. Assume armed men looking for an escape route. My team will cover the front and assess the situation. Let's go.' Eve and Rashi sat behind the wheels of two cars which Kate and her team quickly filled.

Five minutes later they approached a single patrol car already blocking one end of the high street, keeping onlookers from entering the danger zone. Another blocked the farthest end whilst a third was slewed across the road twenty metres further down the street. Two constables stood attentively behind the vehicle watching from safety. Eve and Rashi drove smartly around the obstacle in front of them and pulled up smoothly alongside the already stationary vehicle.

Kate gathered her officers around the constables already in situ. 'Quick update please.'

'We believe there to be two men in the shop Ma'am plus possibly three hostages, that is two staff and one customer.'

Thoughts and options were buzzing around her head. She had been here before and her experience told her to take a deep breath and allow her ever heightening senses to absorb the scene. It was funny how in these situations your hearing became keener, your sight took in more detail, even the smells were stronger, and time, passed more slowly. 'How do you know?' asked Kate.

'Well to be honest Ma'am we heard the alarm go off and went to investigate but when we walked in the door, we were confronted by two men with guns. One of them was pointing his weapon at a lady Ma'am. Not proud Ma'am but we legged it back out the door and raised the alarm.'

'That's okay constable you did the right thing. Now concentrate on keeping people out of our way and we'll take care of this crap.'

'One more thing Ma'am.' The second constable interrupted Kate's flow and she began to chew slowly. 'Those thieves could have just walked past us with those guns Ma'am and we wouldn't have been able to stop them, so why didn't they?'

It was a good point, but the answer was obvious to Kate. She didn't feel the time was right to explain that both the officers and the robbers had panicked. The best result would have been for them to walk away, they could have been caught later with no threat to life. Now there was a very big threat. Action was needed and it had to be quick, the longer such a situation went on without contact the more nerves would fray. There was no obvious action taking place inside. She would have to move forward. She had need of more information to help her consider the possible outcomes. Before Kate could finish her deliberations two figures appeared on the street outside the under siege jewellers. One was a tall, slim guy, his features hidden inside a hoodie, the other was a middle aged woman small but plump, a look of abject terror imprinted on her face.

'Listen, I don't want no trouble, this wasn't meant to happen.' He turned to the frightened female in his grip. 'Tell them I ain't hurt you, I ain't threatened you.'

The poor woman couldn't speak, instead she burst out in tears, sobbing uncontrollably. Kate stepped forward.

'It's okay, I believe you, we can sort this out very easily. Put down your gun let the lady go and we can go from there.' Her training was asserting itself at exactly the right time. Preservation of life, the first duty in any operation. She took a quick glance in each direction noting the positions of her officers. Her gaze fell for a fleeting moment on DS Kendall who looked so calm, so serene but the look was also edged with an aura of dark determination. She took solace from the fact that her team were all hunkered down, all relatively safe. That left two more hostages and another potential gunman to account for. They all mattered if it came to a body count.

Sweat was pouring from the gunman's face his eyes red with stress, his hand starting to shake. 'It ain't that easy, you don't understand, it's not what it looks like.'

Kate pondered his remarks analysing their meaning, searching between the lines for the openings that would allow her to negotiate. Without warning DI Lewis strode out from behind a car moving smartly past Kate. She made to catch his arm, but he swerved her and moved slowly toward the thief.

'Is that you Carl?' Damian's intervention caught the gunman by surprise. Holding his hands up he let his hostage slip from his grasp but made no attempt to stop her running toward the officer. Damian wrapped his arms around the woman as DS Kendall seemed to appear from nowhere and taking the woman by the arm, ushered her to safety.

'Damian man, get away he'll shoot you man.' He glanced nervously back to the shop front.

Lewis lowered his voice so nobody else could hear. 'Carl, mate please, I don't know what's gone down here but when I say go, aim the gun away from me, take five very big paces to the right, lay down and push the gun away from you. Trust me mate.' Damian signalled behind his back to his colleagues, a downward sweep of his hand to signal calm.

Carl was totally unprotected without his hostage, but he clearly feared for his friend. 'He's mad, honestly he'll shoot you Damian.'

'Let me worry about that bro'. On my word we move.' Damian was suddenly starting to feel the pressure, not quite sure what had propelled him forward when he realised who the gunman was, a schoolboy friend, like him a good lad at heart, from a smashing family. Damian felt he was in a dream, his words, spoken with such authority, struck him as not his own, his actions, definitely not, but he had come too far, the would be hero had to carry this thing through. Suddenly he was aware of the sounds around him and he found it disconcerting. The light seemed brighter and colours more vivid.

Damian's thoughts returned to the plight of his friend. He spoke with his eyes, questioning the man's readiness. He received the response he wanted and without further delay, nodded, and yelled. 'Go!'

Both men suddenly leapt in the same direction landing flat on the floor. Within seconds three more police officers were alongside them, two cuffing the villain of the piece while Tess made sure Damian wasn't hurt. Kate meanwhile edged toward the shop, weapon ready. Within heartbeats Rashi was behind her. All was silent. Something was wrong. 'We've got to go in. On my count hit the door and roll. One, two, three.'

With no time to think Rashi swept forward hurtling through the door hitting the floor and sweeping low. Kate followed hot on his heels, gun held high. They were confronted by two petrified faces staring back at them, mouths firmly taped, hands tied roughly with cord. The woman nearest to them indicated wildly with her head directing the officers' attention to an open rear door. Tess and DC Lewis flew in through the open front door as Kate rushed after the missing hostage taker. She returned within minutes. 'Well gone, and no sign of bloody DI Kruse.' Kate turned to DC Lewis her look one of mixed emotions. 'You and I will talk later.'

Without warning Kate's radio sparked into life. The voice of Trent Kruse, clearly stressed, came over loud and clear. 'We've been stuck in traffic Kate, two of us are running to the scene now. I will radio you when we are in position.'

Kate sighed. 'It's all over, we have one offender in custody but the other escaped out the back. Three hostages secure and apart from being scared shitless they are okay. My team will escort the prisoner back to the station. I will wait here until you can get back to the front of the shop and then leave you to preserve the scene, call in forensics and organise full support for the three we rescued. DS Kendall has already taken a description of the second man from our prisoner and she has left it with Constable Markham who is on scene. Liaise with him and then follow this up with a further description from the hostages, to confirm the one we have, before establishing their wellbeing and taking full statements. In that order, please, and get your men canvassing the area now. See if you can call in any air support to help the hunt.'

Kate was well aware her instructions would grate with a fellow DI because if the situation was reversed, they would get right up her nose. She didn't enjoy doing it, but she was the officer in charge and that was how it had to be.

Kate's senses were returning to near normal although she could still feel and hear her heart pounding while her fingers tingled as the adrenalin flow relaxed. She now had to consider how she would phrase the debriefing she would have to undergo with Ratclifffe. She thought through the events that had just flashed past. A blur of action. She realised they did not reflect too well on the operation. A DC disobeying her orders, putting both lives and the mission at risk, an armed criminal escaping easily through a back door. It didn't look good and it certainly didn't feel good. She considered the positives. One robber captured, nobody hurt, three hostages released safely. On another day that would have been a result. She could cover DC Lewis' actions easily enough, but allowing an armed man to simply walk out the back door, the back bloody door of all things. It was DI Kruse's fault. No, she was in charge. It was down to the traffic. She should have considered that. Kate bit her bottom lip stared up at the sky and pronounced on her findings. 'Shit.'

By the time Kate arrived back at the station Ratcliffe's summons was ready to be passed on, by the Desk Sergeant. Bill Cater was as you would expect, a stout man in his fifties, seen it all done it all, no longer capable of either. He was however normally fairly sympathetic and a great reader of situations.

'DCS Ratcliffe would like the pleasure of your company Ma'am.' His words were spoken in a friendly tone and then Sergeant Carter always spoke that way.

'And do you think it will be a pleasure, Sarge?'

He rolled his eyes and shrugged. 'I've seen him looking happier and I've seen him looking less concerned but overall, I got the impression he was slightly relieved. But you know the Chief Super

Ma'am, he will find something to moan about. In my opinion, for what it's worth, it sounds like you did a damn good job Kate.'

Kate smiled at the praise. If only he knew the half of it, which unfortunately, Ratcliffe would.

She made her way to the fourth floor, each step becoming more leaden the closer she came to her debrief. Her phone began to sparkle into life, her ringtone based on Beethoven's Ode to Joy seemed somehow inappropriate. Should she answer? She did. 'DI Taylor.'

'Kate have you seen the Chief yet?' It was DI Trent Kruse somewhat breathless and possibly excited.

'No, that pleasure awaits me in ten metres time, so you had better make it quick.'

'You might say it's good news Kate, especially for me. The hostages have told me the second man left before the first one emerged from the jewellers. Apparently, he said he was going upstairs to get a better view of the police, but the witnesses are absolutely certain he went straight out the back leaving his 'mate' to face the music alone. They are also pretty sure the guy we arrested had no idea his accomplice had left the shop because he was so nervous, and extremely eager to put an end to the whole thing. They reckon he seemed unable to take everything in.'

'Trent that is good news you might just have saved my bacon. See you later for a full overview and to plan the way forward.' Kate switched off her phone and breathed a huge sigh of relief because she now had all the bases covered.

With renewed confidence Kate knocked on the door which once open would expose her to a grilling which a few minutes ago was going to leave her rather exposed. She had her thoughts together and the line of events properly catalogued in her brain. If Ratcliffe asked the right questions she might come out of this on the positive side. The memory that an armed man was loose on the streets, however, still haunted her, and in that state of mind she entered the lion's den.

To her surprise Ratcliffe was standing beside his desk. This was not normal, a desk was there to form a barrier. Kate's eyes narrowed suspiciously as she subconsciously prepared herself to duck.

'Are you alright Kate?' The suspicion grew, no desk, first names. She sucked her lip. 'Yes Sir, thank you Sir.

'From what I have heard so far you and your team did a splendid job today. Everybody safe. That's a result, well done.' Ratcliffe paused. Kate recognised the method, praise, criticise, praise in that order. She knew what was coming next and braced herself.

'One of the criminals escaped Kate. What happened?'

'It would appear he used his "partner" to cover his escape Sir. According to the hostages he disappeared before we were in position.' At this point Kate wasn't prepared to divulge full details especially if they could be seen as any sort of failure.

'Right. Okay.' Ratcliffe clearly wanted to take this on further but didn't appear to know how to. 'Very well DI Taylor.' Kate noticed first names had been dropped. 'Full report as a priority but in the meantime, what are you going to do about the one that got away?'

'I will have someone trawling through the CCTV coverage of the area plus I have instructed DI Kruse to canvass the streets for leads Sir.'

'Find him quickly, he's armed and therefore dangerous. He mustn't be allowed to remain at large for any longer than necessary. I want you to stay in charge of this one Kate but make full use of DI Kruse and continue with your existing agenda.' Ratcliffe moved back behind his desk and opened a file without any further reference to Kate. Obviously, the meeting was at and end. Kate had no wish to prolong it and headed for the door relieved at the outcome, grateful for the time to get her "ducks in a row".

Kate had a number of priorities, have a "chat" to DC Lewis,

allocate someone to CCTV duty and catch up with DI Kruse. She also had to revisit the meeting cut short by the hostage drama. 'Stay in charge.' Kate found herself muttering again. 'Continue with your existing agenda.' Her face was changing expression as she repeated Ratcliffe's words. For a moment she was in a world of her own, oblivious to the strange looks being cast in her direction by officers on route to her office. Kate stormed through the open plan area and on noticing DC Lewis at his desk let it all out. 'Lewis my office. Now.'

Damian shivered, rubbed his face between his hands and took his time to face the consequences of his recent actions. Delay would either give her time to calm down or rile her even more, he hoped it would be the former.

'Sit down. I'm going to say this in private DC Lewis as I have no desire to humiliate you in front of your colleagues.' Damian knew better than to interrupt a DI Taylor rant. 'Once we have had this discussion no more will be said about it. That might be because you are no longer in my team. Do you understand DC Lewis?'

Damian was taken aback by the threat. He had expected a rollicking, a warning probably, but thrown out of the team, no way. His mind was reeling but he had to ride this one out, stay calm, take it on the chin. 'Yes Ma'am.'

Kate saw the effect her words were having, the effect they were meant to have. Time to turn the screw, not too little, not too much. Lessons had to be learnt, for young coppers the harsher the better.

'Did you disobey my strict instructions DC Lewis?' Kate did not pause for an answer. 'In doing so, do you understand you risked the lives of yourself, your fellow officers and the hostages DC Lewis? How do you think you would have felt if somebody had been killed? What do you think your colleagues would have thought of you if somebody had been killed? Do you think you would be sat here having this talk if somebody had been killed?'

Kate was applying the pressure with a staccato of statements designed to confuse as much as to get an answer. She didn't want his answers, she wanted to drown him in remorse, in guilt, in fear. Perhaps then he would never repeat the same mistake.

Damian sat slumped, shocked by the barrage, his mind a whirl, all confidence sapped. Raising his head, resignation written in his eyes he forced himself to ask a question, any question to stop the onslaught. 'Will I be suspended Ma'am?'

Enough damage had been done, the cruelty could stop. 'If I was going to suspend you it wouldn't just be the two of us here, would it Lewis. As it happens it doesn't suit my needs to suspend you.' Time for a little praise or at least that's what the text book says. 'You acted on instinct Damian.' First names ease the pressure. 'Detective Constables do not act on instinct they act on orders, only officers commanding an operation act on instinct. Have you got that?' Kate continued once again denying Damian the chance to answer. 'You may act on instinct if you ever find yourself in a tricky situation on your own, and only if the orders you have been given cannot be carried out. Do you understand.' This time there was opportunity for a reply.

'Yes Ma'am.'

'Damian what you did was brave, your solution to an exceedingly difficult situation was perhaps not considered but it was effective. You kept your nerve once you were committed and quite probably you saved lives. This time. Now this is what will happen. From now on, you will receive nothing but praise from me for your actions in front of your team. You will accept any praise coming your way. Nothing will be said about you disobeying orders, ever. You've had your "slap" and you've taken it like a man. Let's see if we can make a real officer of you.'

'I don't know what to say Ma'am.' Damian began to splutter his genuine thanks, an attempt cut immediately short.

'What do you not understand about "it's over" DC Lewis. Come on we have a meeting to attend.' Kate strode swiftly from her office leaving DC Lewis in her wake. He rushed after her tripping over first a waste basket and then the chord of the desk lamp bringing it crashing to the floor.

'Holy shit' thought Lewis.

'Brilliant' thought Kate as she continued on her way.

Kate had requested the attendance of DI Kruse at the debrief meeting. She would get that out of the way, issue instructions allowing the search for the missing gunman to progress, and then get back to putting some bastards behind bars. She had decided to put Tess Campbell in charge of the CCTV. She appeared to be thorough, intelligent but not so hot on the team stuff. That would have to change but for now Kate would use it in her favour. There was little left of the day, the meeting would eat up the remaining time and more. No night patrol tonight she decided, clean start in the morning.

10. Eve's Folly

Eve sat sprawled in front of the telly. She had decided on a bottle of Chablis to go with her micro waved curry. No Kings Arms tonight just her and Brad Pitt. But first the local news. She couldn't bring herself to listen to the national channels, no news just opinion, nothing upbeat only criticism of whatever the latest flavour happened to be.

She sipped her wine, cold, white, and dry. It reminded her of Burgundy, her favourite holiday haunt. She closed her lips around a spoonful of rice. That didn't have the same effect. She had missed the news headlines, but it was only background noise anyway. Eve was tired. She knew it was a reaction to the frustration she was feeling with the lack of progress at work. She thrived on results, lived for the dispensing of justice, and fell into depression when neither inhabited her life.

The phone rang, she ignored it at first, playing a silly game with herself. She knew she would answer.

'Eve? It's Harry.' Eve put down her glass. Which particular team was short tonight she wondered?

'You know I'm crap at darts Harry, always make a right fool of myself.'

'Have you seen the news Eve?'

'Well it's on, but no not really.'

'A young girl has gone missing Eve, and Eve it's Terry Frost's kid. He's on his way here Eve, he's looking for you.'

'Harry it's not my bag at the moment, I'm involved in something else, surely he's been interviewed by somebody at the station.' Eve was feeling slightly sick. She didn't want this added stress. Images flickered across her vision, at the same time clouding her mind. 'I'm on my way Harry but they will have designated officers to the case, I'll talk with him but that's about it.'

'You're an angel, thanks Eve I'll have your lager waiting for you.'

'I've got a feeling it's going to take more than that Harry, much more.'

Eve drained her glass took another mouthful of spicy chicken and placed the plate on the kitchen table. Just another unfinished meal for yet another different reason.

Ten minutes later and Eve was taking an unexpected sip of her beer. She had arrived before Frost and picked out one of the two tables where conversation was not likely to be overheard. She felt uncomfortable about this meeting and her instincts rarely let her down. This time she didn't listen to them.

Terry Frost arrived clearly distraught, undeniably angry and sweating under pressure. Frost came straight to the table and sat down opposite Eve. 'Thanks for meeting me Eve.'

Eve stopped him in his tracks. 'It's DS Kendall tonight Mr Frost and before we go any further why aren't you down at the police station giving them as much information as you can about your daughter's disappearance.'

'I've already spent hours with them and I'm on my way back. Honest Eve, I mean DS Kendall, I just don't have any faith in them, but I do know, you wouldn't stop till you found her. I know about you see.'

Eve's face distorted in anger before she leaned over to within inches of Frosts face. 'You know absolutely nothing about me Frost and if you give me any more shit, you can take a hike.'

Terry Frost paled. This woman had an edge, something dark, something deep and when whatever it was surfaced, he had the impression it was best not to be around.

'Sorry, really sorry. Please help me. I know who's got her. It's that bastard pervert from the other day down at the swimming pool. If I catch him, I'm going to kill him Eve.' Frost made no effort to correct himself this time. Eve sat back removing the confrontation zone. This was becoming such a pain.

'You are not going to do anything of the sort you are going straight back to the station and you will continue with this through the proper channels.'

Terry Frost sighed, appearing to consider his threats. He reached into his jacket pocket and brought out a nasty looking knife shielded by a brown leather sheaf. 'You'd better take this then.' He offered the knife to her, handle first.

'Bloody hell.' Exclaimed Eve moving to take the knife, gripping the handle, but before she could take control of it Frost snatched it back. 'How do I know you won't just charge me for possession of a dangerous weapon.'

'I'll tell you what Mr Frost, you think about it. I need another drink. One for you?'

'Just a shot of scotch please, then I'll be off down the station.'

Eve stepped over to the bar shaking her head in disbelief. Harry looked at her enquiringly. 'Don't ask' ordered Eve with a look that brooked no dissent. 'Pint for me, small scotch for him.'

She heard Frost's phone ring and saw his face light up. Pushing back his chair he rushed to the bar.

'She's back, it's over. 'I'm so sorry I've been a total jerk. I shouldn't have bothered you but believe me you have been so helpful, you've put me back on track.' He grabbed the scotch Harry had placed on the bar emptied it down his throat and ran out the door.

Eve and Harry looked at each other their faces both pictures of disbelief. 'While you're here Eve we are one short for the darts tonight.' Harry smiled sneakily.

Eve laughed 'You old bastard. The drinks are most certainly on you tonight.'

11. The Only Way Is Up

Tess Campbell was delighted to have been given the task of examining the CCTV of the recent operation. She was determined to track down the gunmen who had fled the scene. This was real policing. She had wanted to start immediately but DI Taylor insisted everybody went home, relaxed and came back with a new vigour and renewed focus on their main job.

Tess had other things to keep her busy anyway. She was determined to get as far up the ladder as possible and would do anything to make her ambitions a reality. To that end she had enrolled in the Open University. She already had a degree in psychology and now she was studying law. Tess still hadn't decided which branch of the police force she would end up in but right now she quite liked the idea of forensics. Being a "fast track" officer she knew her prospects were bright, and she was going to open any, and every door she could, if it profited her. She remembered her dad's words again "Don't let anyone stand in your way girl." Tess wasn't really sure how far she would take that advice only time would tell.

She had a smart, contemporary flat. It had taken a while to have it decorated but now it was looking almost the way she wanted it. Two bedrooms, built in wardrobes, pale shades of beige and a walk in shower in the one she used. Open plan. The lounge area she had furnished with two anonymous sofas, colour added through extravagant vases and pictures adorning the walls. There were just one or two imperfections she was unhappy with. The walnut colour in the bathroom could have been a little bit lighter, the lamp in the corner somehow didn't quite meet expectations, and the oven, she should have gone for a double oven. And the view. That would have to change. She would be moving onward and upwards very soon, then she would have a view.

She had a boyfriend. He proved useful on occasions. She hadn't felt the need for an "occasion" for a while now, she hadn't had the time or the inclination. He was fairly successful, not bad looking, earned a decent wage. He made her laugh and they had many things in common except one, he didn't have her drive. He would have to change. Tess thought for a minute. He would have to be changed for someone better.

Tess had a career. She had believed she was going to go far. She had the intelligence, the qualifications, the intent. She needed the experience and she required a helping hand. Her new assignment had been seen as a retrograde step until she met Jonathan Ratcliffe. Now it suited her plans perfectly.

Damian had a room. It was cosy and part of a house he had grown up in. It housed all his worldly belongings and more importantly his memories. He would get around to decorating it someday. He should decorate the whole house, he knew that, but he just never seemed to have the time. Still for now he liked his room and he was happy.

Tonight he was slumped in his favourite chair. Bob Marley was playing in the background. He liked all the modern rap stuff, but Marley made him feel chilled, reminded him of who he was. He was only now beginning to feel the backlash. It had been a hell of a day. Surely it had been two days since he had sauntered into the office that morning. Suddenly he wanted to cry. A wisp of a tear came to his eye, his nose twitched, and his lips began to quiver.

He questioned himself, not sure of what was happening. He certainly hadn't expected this reaction. Was it DI Taylor's bollocking? She had been hard but fair. No, he had been stupid he had acted with no thought for himself, only for his "friend". Another day and he would be in the morgue maybe a few others alongside him. What would his mum do, his little sister? The tears came flooding bringing a promise to himself that he would, never, ever, repeat today's stupidity and reducing the flow to a slowly subsiding sob.

12. Into The Fire

He laughed as much from relief as anything else. He lifted his face to the sun and let it drench him. That had been close, too close. To be caught would have been a disaster. He continued to run hoping he had gained himself enough time to get clear of any search. He knew where he was going but he had to slow down once he hit the main roads, too many cameras. He had to think smart, blend in, walk on, disappear, get back to work.

Matei Dacic could not help himself, he was a chancer, easily bored, the night job wasn't enough to absorb his energy. The money they paid him was good, but it was the bosses who were creaming in the big bucks. He should be a boss, he would be a boss, he just needed the right break and he would be the main man for once, the one doing the shouting instead of the bowing and scraping.

He was hot, in need of a drink. A sign, "The Huntsman" loomed large. Matei laughed to himself, it was fate. He sat himself in a dark corner and removed his jacket. A pint of lager frothed over the beer mat and slid across the table. His mind slowed, his body relaxed, but his hands trembled. It was midday. He would stay for an hour or so and then get back. He hadn't been seen and so he would have nothing to explain. He reached into his jacket pocket pulling out three small velvet covered boxes each the home to awfully expensive rings. It hadn't been a complete waste of time, it was a classy jewellers, these were worth maybe a grand.

They would ask where he had been, they always did. They made it seem like just friendly interest, but it wasn't, it was pure control. He would have to say something, he always had to. Matei's answer was always to stop at the Polish shop and buy some sausage and maybe some potato bread. That was what he always did. It never failed.

The walls were damp in places, the paint flaking from the crumbling plaster. The windows were small. They let the light in but nothing out. Iron bars added to the security. The floors were laid with old grey, cold tiles, here and there a small puddle, the result of water dripping from the ceiling. There many corridors, many claustrophobic, badly lit rooms. Each of these rooms housed a bed complete with soiled mattress, small tables, their tops home to empty bottles and broken syringes. Many had an armchair, stuffing peering through long worn fabric of a now indescribable colour. It was a depressing scene part of a depressing life.

In most of these rooms could be spied a figure, usually curled up, sleeping. These apparitions were dirty, bruised, uninterested in their appearance, lost souls bereft of a future. Andrei Micalovic entered one such room, a girl stirred, her flimsy dress slipping from her shoulder.

'Wake up you have work to do in a couple of hours.' The girl responded slowly to the Slavic request, her eyes flitting in and out of oblivion whilst her limbs stretched themselves, automatically obeying her master's voice.

Micalovic moved on to the next room. His partner Adi Petrovic would be performing the same duties on the floor above. Neither would be aware of the suffering, neither would care even if they were. Their enterprise was buying them land and property at home and they would put up with the low life they were leading now for a much brighter future later. Andrei heard sudden screams. Adi was handling the goods again. He couldn't understand why anyone would want to touch these girls let alone pay to use them, but they did. Every night except Sunday. He considered their customers to be devils, dirty old men, perverts of the worst sort especially if the stories the girls told were anything to go by. His face scowled, if anyone did such things to his daughters, he would make them eat their own balls before he flayed them alive.

In stark contrast to the way the two men used the girls, they treated their "employees" like family. They had twelve of the hardest looking, mean spirited bastards money could buy on their "payroll". They were paid well both for their ruthless control of customers and girls alike and for their complete loyalty to Petrovic and Micalovic. For sure, now and again the two partners would have to make an example of one of their men but only when really necessary. Today had been such a time, a fool jeopardising the operation for the sake of a few extra dollars, as if these men weren't paid enough for their work. Break the rules you get broken, a cut to the throat, a trip down the river. But no, more often than not it was the girls who had to be reminded of the hopelessness of attempting to escape. Today for whatever reason was a busy day for lessons to be learned.

The girls were being herded into the room that served as their kitchen, over twenty of them packed in, avoiding the grease. Some sat at the long formica tables others perched themselves on the kitchen tops. One was missing but not for long.

The young woman they knew as Lottie was suddenly thrust through the door, headfirst, her brow acting as a battering ram for the swing doors. Adi Petrovic flung her to the floor before kicking her violently in the stomach. Lottie doubled up in pain. Her cut and bleeding hands clutching her battered ribs. Both eyes were swollen and almost completely closed, her nose twisted to one side, her lips split so many times. Petrovic dragged her up by the hair and slammed her face into a tabletop scattering the girls sitting there.

'You see what she is making me do, you see how she is making me suffer? Why did you do this Lottie? Why betray your family? Why haven't you learned from the other girls, the other examples we have been forced to make of those who disrespect us.' Several of the young women present were beginning to cry, fearfully trying to stifle their sobbing in case Petrovic turned his attention on them. He didn't like to be interrupted on such occasions as this.

'You know what she has done eh!' Nobody answered. 'She tried to leave us. How many times have I told you? You are free to go when we are finished, not before. And now this.' The man shook his head. 'You make me weep Lottie.'

'Goran.' A giant human being entering the room, a wicked looking blade on one hip, a pistol on the other. 'Take her she is yours and when you have finished anyone's, and when they have finished, get rid of her.'

Lottie was dragged away, screaming through broken teeth and tattered lips to a fate made obvious by their owner. 'Get back to your rooms and make yourself presentable. Bogdan will be around later if you should want something to help you through the night.' The girls shuffled past him before walking as fast as possible back to their cells, running was not allowed. Most would accept something from the "Doctor" as Bogdan was known, anything to block out the realities of their miserable existence.

The cars would draw up around eight o'clock, six nights a week. The girls would sit, lie, wait. A figure would appear in the doorway. Why never a smile accompanying it. The girls could hope for nothing more than a degree of decency from their visitor. It was rarely the case. The fumbling began. The slap, why was that so much a part of the ritual? Did it make the beast more of a man? The obnoxious grunts, the disgusting warmth within, perhaps another slap. A silent retreat, another short wait, another never ending nightmare about to begin.

13. The Mole

Kate made an early start striding past the Desk Sergeant who was sleepily coming to the end of his shift. There was always something weird about ships in the night". Kate existed in the Sergeant's life pattern and vice versa, just "there", nothing more nothing less, no further knowledge of each other than a morning "hello". Kate's thoughts were interrupted by a deep voice from behind the desk.

'Morning Kate.'

'Hello Sarge.'

Kate moved on. As her mind returned from its musings, she looked up to see Tess Campbell slipping into the lift. Running after her she failed to beat the closing doors. Waiting patiently, she watched the lift reach and pass their first floor, the second floor was missed the lift not stopping until the fourth floor. Kate's brain was performing somersaults and she determined to follow her colleague. Taking the steps two at a time She flew up to the fourth floor in record time. Tess stood waiting outside the closed door of DCS Ratcliffe. Kate positioned herself to watch, half hidden by a tall loping palm. Seconds later the door was opened, and DC Campbell was ushered in.

'My mole?' muttered Kate to herself before following the stairs back down to the first floor.

It wasn't long before DC Campbell appeared and sat down at her desk. She seemed oblivious to Kate's presence as she switched on her computer and looked for the CCTV footage loaded up the night before.

'You're in nice and early Tess.' Kate's voice was friendly, her smile genuine enough. 'Just arrived?' That was the giveaway, the extra question that posed the menace. An experienced officer would have picked up on it. Tess didn't.

'Yes Ma'am eager to get on with finding the runaway.' Tess was good, no nerves showing.

'Thanks again for giving me this opportunity to show what I can do Ma'am.'

'I have total confidence in you DC Campbell, you're a smart girl, a lot to learn, like anybody of your short experience, but I am confident it will come because you are clearly eager to learn. You needn't join in the meeting this morning, prioritise your search, it's important.'

Tess beamed, completely missing the underlying tone that flitted in and out of Kate's questions and statements. Don't "join in the meeting", dead giveaway, totally unheeded.

Kate bit her lip, turned, and headed to her own sanctuary well aware that if Tess was the "mole" she was bloody good at it.

'Right.' Kate was focused. She had to get her team back out there and quickly.

The meeting had been ongoing for several hours interrupted only by a few breaks for nature and drinks. Sandwiches would be delivered soon. The team had combined their findings from the preliminary canvassing and stake out. The thing that stood out was the talk of the activity to the east of town and the lack of it elsewhere. Kate was eager to wrap things up before lunch and get her team back out on the streets. She could then catch up with DC Campbell and DI Kruse.

The door barged open. 'Sorry meant to knock first.' Tess was flushed both from embarrassment and excitement. Before she could be invited to explain herself her news came blurting out.

'I've tracked the other gunman Ma'am.'

'Great give us the details then DC Campbell.'

'I've been able to track him from the street adjoining the rear entrance of the shop, through the town to the metro. I've been through the CCTV at all the stops his train was passing through, and picked him up again at, guess where Ma'am.'

Kate glared at Tess, she was in no mood for games after too many hours in a stuffy office. She wanted answers because at the moment they were few and far between.

Tess frowned unintentionally. DI Taylor could be such a bore sometimes. She quickly recovered her composure and continued her report. 'Parklands Ma'am. I have him getting off and leaving the station from which he enters a pub called the Huntsman. Problem is Ma'am we don't see him come out. What's more although we have some good clear footage of his face, we can't match him from our files.'

'An illegal then.' Rashi confirmed everyone's thoughts. Unfortunate, there was no identifying the suspect, but at least his movements tied in nicely with the canvassing results.

'Well done Tess, good work and achieved in extra quick time.' Kate's genuine praise brought a broad smile to the face of DC Campbell who liked nothing more than a pat on the back and some encouraging words.

The door opened yet again. This time it was the sandwiches. Kate lifted an egg roll from the tray, took a bite, chewed vigorously, and swallowed, all the time formulating her next orders.

'After lunch Tess, you and Rashi take a visit to the Huntsmen, speak to the bar staff and get hold of the CCTV. We need to know where this guy went, whether he spoke to anybody, as much information as possible about the way he looked, spoke, behaved. Eve will you partner Damian and take a daytime look at the kebab shop in Roche. Put some fresh eyes on it and Damian compare the night time activity you experienced with what you see this afternoon.'

Kate felt strangely refreshed, her torrent of words acting like a valve. They were back in the game an unexpected robbery having an unexpected connection to their main operation no matter how tenuous it might be.

'Don't rush your lunch but don't dawdle either.' Kate snatched another roll not even bothering to check its contents and headed for the exit. 'I'm clocking in on DI Kruse to update him with your findings Tess and to see if he has anything that we can add to them.'

Kate arrived at the office of DI Kruse just in time to see him disappearing down the corridor. 'Trent hang on a minute I have some important news.'

'Me too Kate. Join me if you like I'm on the way to the river. There's a body being dragged out. We can catch up on the way. Kate pondered the invite. Was this another distraction. She quickly made her decision, distraction or not she needed to speak with DI Kruse, and a body in the river, no brainer.

The drive to the river would normally take fifteen minutes or so giving Kate and DI Kruse precious time to share any new findings relevant to the missing gunmen. It was nice not to be behind the wheel for a change and Kate spent the first few moments noticing those things you just don't see when you are focused on the road. She noted one or two new shops and wondered how long they had been open, a new film being advertised on a rather spectacular hoarding, another Costa Coffee to compete with the never ending rows of cafes already dominating the streets of Loxborough.

'We've not had much luck with the canvassing around the jewellers I'm afraid Kate. Seems half the people who live around the incident were out of their houses milling around the front of the shops trying to get a look at the action. Any suggestions for a better use of resources?'

'Obviously, I want my guys concentrating on our main task of crushing the threat to our young girls, however, we have had a bit of a break. I have had DC Campbell trawling through the CCTV and the clever so and so has found clear footage which my officers are checking out right now. They are concentrating on a pub where he appears to have gone to ground, or, found a way out not covered by the cameras. Bad news is despite the clear images of the suspect we can't match him to any files. We have sent you some of the stills so please circulate them amongst your officers and let's see what transpires. I haven't had a good look myself, but I do have a copy for you to take a gander at later on.'

'Frustrating' murmured DI Kruse. 'Seems to be the story of the aftermath of this case.'

Di Kruse brought the car to a halt twenty metres from the site of a remarkably busy retrieval operation. A white tent had already been erected a short distance from the river, while police crime tape divided the area into several different zones. Figures in white forensic gowns busied themselves in the pursuit of a set procedure and divers still dotted the water and its banks, occasionally disturbing the wildlife resulting in a flurry of leaves and spray.

'Hi Kate, Trent.' They were greeted by Helen Gates, a small lady, grey whispering through her otherwise short, dark curly hair. Here was a serious woman, the main CSI for any high importance forensics in the area. She was good, exceptionally good, and luckily for the crime teams extremely helpful. Helen combined her exceptional scientific talents with a huge desire to see criminals brought to justice.

'Initial findings Helen?' Trent Kruse was the first to answer Helen's greeting.

'Male, in his mid thirties, eastern European by the look of the features you can see, but don't quote me on that at this stage. Possibly tortured or maybe sadistically "played with" before having his throat slit and his body dumped in the river. Two broken legs, one arm, jaw, an eye poked out and multiple bruising. Time of death difficult to tell as he's been in the river. Give me a few hours and I'll get back to you. If we can get an idea of the time and the ebbing of the river, we just might be able to tell with some small degree of accuracy where he was thrown in.'

'That would be great if we could do that Helen. Can we take a look?' It was Kate who posed the question.

'You can but only once you have kitted up. And chaps it's not a particularly nice sight.' Helen moved over to one of her team busily preparing his camera and after a few quick words they both returned to the body.

The two detectives duly pulled on the necessary anti contamination gowns, shoes, masks, and headgear before cautiously poking their heads around the tent entrance. Kate stood back. This was DI Kruse's case. He didn't linger. Water had a way of doing disturbing things to a body. Inevitably he turned away showing a natural distaste for the scene before him.

'I think I'll wait for the forensics report.' Trent drew back with an involuntary shudder, his face somewhat paler than it had been when they had entered the enclosed space. It must be bad if an old hand like Kruse was affected so badly. Kate allowed him to pass and stepped closer to the body. She had no idea what she was looking for, she never did on these occasions, but she knew if there were answers to be found here, they would eventually leap out at her. Everyone worked differently, most would have a mental process they would exhaust in their search for clues. Kate didn't look for them they just came. Something about his clothes registered in her mind but she couldn't grasp what. And then it did. His jacket, a not unusual denim, however a rather rare badged stared back at her. Kate rushed back to the car returning with the photo she had left with DI Kruse.

'It's him, it's bloody him. Trent look.'

Di Kruse took the picture from Kate. 'Bloody hell Kate the poor guy in there has his face battered you can't possibly identify him as the bloke in that photo.'

Kate leaned over Trent's shoulder. 'Not the face, it's the badge.'

DI Kruse looked again. 'CFR Cluj. It's a sodding football team. Kate that's no way a coincidence. Brilliant Kate, that's our man.'

'My man Trent. He's related to my case and this is my dead body now.'

DI Kruse took it in good humour and the two of them hastened back to the station desperate to get more detailed information from forensics. The time of death, the flow of the tide, the place the body entered the water. Crack the first two and the third fell into line and Kate would be able to close in on the killers and perhaps answer a fistful of questions.

DS Kamani and DC Campbell were waiting in the office when Kate and Trent Kruse walked through the door. 'Afternoon Ma'am I'm afraid we didn't get much from the Huntsman.' Rashi began but Tess interrupted. 'Barman said he remembered serving the man, but he was busy so had no idea of how or when he left.'

Rashi regained control. 'There is a doorway out the back, one or two private security cameras dotted about the lane so we'll see if we can bring in the footage. Other than that, not too helpful Ma'am.' He looked slightly despondent, but Kate's update would rekindle his spirits.

'It's a good job DI Kruse and I have been out and about then isn't it. We've found our man. Slight problem. He's dead. Good news is forensics might be able to pinpoint the area in which he was killed, and Tess, it's almost certainly Parklands.'

Rashi and Tess locked eyes, the team were back in business. 'When will we know Ma'am?' asked Tess.

'Tomorrow morning DC Campbell, and then the real work

begins.'

It was the smile that caught everybody's attention. It could only mean one thing. Progress. Helen Gates strode up to Kate's door and knocked once, before entering without waiting. Without exception the team looked agonisingly after her, desperate for news. DI Taylor's door opened as quickly as it had closed, and the two women emerged together.

'Okay team let's hear this together. What have you got Helen?'

'Your man is, as I think you know Kate, of eastern European descent. He was brutally beaten and finally killed with a knife cut to the throat. He was then dumped into the river immediately after. The approximate time of his death was yesterday between fifteen hundred and sixteen hundred hours. He was, therefore, in the water, again an estimate, for up to eighteen hours. Unfortunately, the river would have ebbed and flowed more than once during this period so we cannot ascertain from this where he was placed into the water.'

All four officers sighed, each one wondering, without saying anything, why on earth this woman had been so bloody happy when she arrived. They didn't have to wait long to understand.

'But here's the good news. We are pretty damn certain he met his death on or near to the Parklands Industrial Estate. And how do we know this I hear you ask?'

Her audience were in the palm of her hand and Helen Gates was loving this moment, she always did. It was her time for centre stage and every time it happened, she made damned sure she soaked up the atmosphere. She continued.

'Criminals on the whole are pretty dumb. When it comes to big heists, there are some clever buggers out there, but when its sheer violence that's involved, brain dead thugs.' Helen paused for effect. It worked.

'Helen please, spit it out.'

'You wouldn't want to ruin my fun, would you Kate?' She smiled, her eyes glinting with mischief. 'These complete morons tried to weigh down the body. They used cement. Now that in itself was quite clever because....'

'Helen for goodness sake.'

'The cement they used would have been in bags. They poured several into a sack and by the look of the marks on the body, tied the sack to his legs. The water would have increased the weight of the cement and Bob's your uncle. We know this because of the marks on the dead man's legs and the fact our clever little divers found the sack. We also know the name of the company to whom the cement belonged, "Hampton & Sons." This company processes its products two miles up river from where the body was found. How do we know this?' Kate glared. 'Okay, the assailants, presumably not wishing to litter the river bank, no doubt purely out of respect for the wildlife, obviously became fed up with emptying the cement into the sack and so simply tore the small bags and put everything in. Clever enough to let the water get at the cement, too lazy to think any further ahead. That's what I call a concrete case.' Helen bowed theatrically.

Everyone looked to Kate for a reaction. Helen meanwhile retained her pose. Kate spoke.

'Thank the lord for stupid criminals. But what the hell is it all about. Robbing a jewellery shop? Taking hostages? Brutal murder?'

'I'm guessing it's time to investigate and destroy Kate?' DI Kruse gave Kate a lopsided look.

'You better believe it Trent. There's a damn sight more to this and we are going to get to the bottom of it. You and me DI Kruse are going for a ride.'

'Ma'am.' Eve Kendall gave them both a questioning look.

'Parklands Industrial Estate. All of you, build a picture, get maps, satellite pictures, check the files, any previous incidents on the site. Find out what companies have units there, research companies house, when did they set up, who are the directors, the shareholders. see if anything stands out that relates to this case. If we aren't back by "knocking" time, meeting tomorrow morning, first thing, have it ready.'

'Kate grabbed her coat and bag from her office and swept past DI Kruse leaving him to pull a face at his colleagues before rushing after DI Taylor.

14. The Breakthrough

The industrial estate was the norm, at least for this part of the country. Hundreds of units set in a square grid, many empty and decaying, a few new buildings under construction, a larger number, well worn, but fully operational.

Kate held her mobile toward DI Kruse pointing out the satellite picture of the layout of Parklands.

'We're here Trent, and there is Hampton and Sons, right next to the river.'

'Wow, that's huge and I didn't even know it was here. Come on Kate let's go see.'

Trent eased the car through the myriad of buildings large and small each road looking more and more like the last one until turning a corner, there straight ahead, was their target. A small road lead down to what was presumably the river. Stopping some forty metres from the water so as not to cause unnecessary damage to any potential evidence left by the killers, the two detectives walked gingerly to the bank.

'God these guys were professional. Not. Look at it Kate, torn cement bags, footmarks and over here, certainly looks like blood. What's the plan Kate, take some photos, bag anything that might go missing and call in forensics, or do you think we need to keep this very much low key?'

Kate mulled the situation over in her mind. The guys who murdered the guy in the river were here on this estate somewhere. She was sure of that, but doing what? She had to balance up losing valuable forensic material against alerting the criminals responsible for the murder.

'We have to follow procedure DI Kruse. We'll take some photos and call forensics in, give them the nod about how delicate this is, and then we are going to need a lucky break.'

Forensics were at the scene within the hour making as much noise as an American Marine Corps on a secret mission. Trent Kruse and DI Taylor cringed.

'That's our first objective missed then. The whole bloody neighbourhood will have heard that, and if they didn't that bloody great marquee and a boat load of police officers in white suits, is certainly going to pique their interest. Let's hope they get some results out of all of this.'

Kate was furious but held her tongue. 'Come on DI Kruse we need to have a good look around the estate for that lucky break. We'll start from the main entrance and do the rounds.' One hour later, minds numbed by touring through roads and buildings all looking the same, the sun glinting through the windscreens, drying their eyes and bathing the car in an uncomfortable warmth, there it was. That lucky break.

'Did you see what I saw Kate?' A faded blue van flashed past their slow moving car.

'No, just a jerk driving too fast, I didn't catch any detail I was looking at the units.'

DI Kruse brought the car to a halt and watched the vehicle continue up the road. 'Three men sat in the cab of the van, Kate. Looked "foreignish", although I was looking at them through the rear mirror. Stuck on their dashboard was a "bobblehead", you know one of those things with a small body and big head that wobbles as you drive. Anyway, I don't know what kit Cluj wear, but the thing in the van was distinctive in so far as it had a diagonal stripe. Unfortunately, I think that is more likely to be associated with South American teams. Anyway, it was a sort of maroon red and white colour. That is quite an unusual combination. Let's have a look.'

Trent googled the Romanian football club. 'Bingo, burgundy and white with a nice diagonal stripe. Try telling me that's a coincidence Kate.'

Kate grinned maniacally. 'Don't just sit there get after them, but slowly, no pretending we're Starsky and Hutch, let's show forensics how it's done.

They followed the road to the end and turned left as the van had done. There was no sign of the van in the long road ahead. Several roads led off to the right. It was going to be a process of elimination. One thing was for sure, this was the rat's end of the estate. These must have been the original plots, most were empty, businesses moving to newer units or moving on all together. Many were shuttered and those that weren't were clearly used only for storage. Even the road on one or two of the side streets seemed to be disappearing into dust tracks. Three streets checked and no sign of the van but the fourth turned up trumps.

'There Trent. Ease up.'

Three hundred metres or so down the road the blue van sat outside a large unit, slightly better maintained than those that surrounded it. Alongside were three other vehicles, all old, well worn, two Mercedes and a grey Volkswagen.

'That's about nine units down. What's this place called?' DI Kruse peered at the weathered sign standing ten metres away. Looks like Stanton Road.'

'Ok let's get back to the main entrance and check out the site plan, see what name they've put alongside this unit.'

Ten minutes later they were looking up at the large signboard located at the entrance to the estate, and soon found the unit they were looking for. There it is,' observed Kate "Star Enterprises". It's still only fifteen hundred hours, I'll call it in and by the time we get back to the station we should have some info. Might be a long night for us DI Kruse.'

'Long and hopefully very interesting DI Taylor.' They smiled at each other and set off for the office.

When they finally appeared in the office her staff were waiting eagerly, clearly excited by the unfolding events. 'What have you found for us guys?'

'Star Enterprises moved into the unit six months ago, pay their rent, rates, utilities through a legit bank account although the amount of money going through that account is minimal. Credit cards are up to date but it's there we see the anomalies.' DS Kendall completed her summary and waited for a response from her superiors. The two Detectives weren't about to play her game and when they didn't oblige, she continued. 'Purchases on the cards are enough to feed an army, food, drink and a great deal of sheets. But this is the interesting bit, the only purchases took place when they moved in and within two weeks they stopped, no more spending.'

'Cash.' Kate and Trent said the word simultaneously and laughed excitedly. 'Brilliant work everybody.'

'Thank you Ma'am.' It had been a team effort, but Tess curtsied theatrically. Kate couldn't help but smile to herself whilst thinking that girl is going to go far if she doesn't get thumped first.

'That seals it then DI Kruse. Grab something to eat and I'll see you back here in a couple of hours.'

Trent Kruse signalled his agreement and left. He would head home for a short break but could hardly control his enthusiasm for the night ahead, this could be big.

'Okay. Now, back to the day job. DS Kendall did you and DC Lewis gain any further insights into the goings on at our kebab shop?'

'Wrong tree and barking up Ma'am. It just doesn't seem to be happening there.' Damian shook his head in clear disappointment and frustration.

'Just because we haven't seen it yet, doesn't mean it's not there DC Lewis.' Eve Kendall would never give up, she was like a dog with a bone, defeat not a word in her vocabulary. 'We need to stay on it Ma'am. The shop could just be a front and the activity could be somewhere else completely. '

'Or inside.' Kate sucked her lip. 'Like you say Eve keep on it for now. Take another look at the satellite of the area, who knows something might jump out.'

15. Confirmation

The run down and derelict looking part of Parklands industrial estate known as Stanton Road was anything but quiet. Watching from their car, strategically placed and well hidden in the shadows, some four hundred metres from the turning into the row of units housing Star Enterprises, DI Taylor and Trent Kruse were completely taken aback by the number of cars, vans and even motorcycles entering the side road.

It had been dimpsy when they arrived, now it was dark, the only light provided by the lamp above the apparent entrance to the building. 'How many do you make that now Trent?'

'It's ridiculous Kate. Thirty bloody two, and we've only been here a couple of hours. It's still only twenty one hundred for goodness sake, and what's more we've yet to see a woman in any of them. But have we seen enough to get a warrant Kate?'

'At the moment we're guessing and that won't be good enough, although there is the body, but I think we need more. Trent take the car and get yourself a proper look, I'll wait here.'

Driving slowly toward the ninth unit on the left hand side of Stanton Road DI Kruse could now see at close hand what was going on at Star Enterprises. There was little light emerging from the building due to the blacked out windows but above a small entrance door set in a dark alcove the red lamp they had seen from the car, cast its dull rays over two burly, club bouncer type, men. Three other men stood in a row, the first handing over what might have been a number of bank notes and in return receiving what appeared to be a raffle ticket, before being allowed to disappear through the door. A second man repeated the process but let his ticket fall from his hand. The "guard" stretched instinctively to catch it and beneath his jacket, Trent caught a glimpse of shining metal.

Swearing to himself he drove past the unit for some twenty metres before turning around and, driving as quickly as possible without drawing too much attention, left the scene. This had just become profoundly serious and potentially extremely dangerous. Trent's observations still might not be enough on their own to ensure a full blown raid, but he was sure he and DI Taylor could be a very persuasive combination.

'This all just became a whole new ball game Kate. Can you see those big gorillas at the front of the building?' He continued without waiting for her response. 'At least one of them is armed, which means it's almost certain they all are. Who knows how many more of these guys there are inside.'

'You're right Trent this is both serious and urgent.'

DI Kruse eased the car away from the scene and headed out of the estate. Kate thought long and hard already compiling in her mind the argument she would be putting to Ratcliffe for immediate action before anyone else was hurt or worse killed. Trent Kruse would want to be in on the meeting. She didn't want that. When it came to a potential argument she liked to work alone. 'I'll arrange a meeting with the boss for mid morning to give us time to put our heads together.'

Trent Kruse nodded happily. Kate smiled at him almost apologetically. She would be in Ratcliffe's office long before that.

The full team had gathered. There were so many things to discuss, to report, to debrief, but overnight the situation at Parklands had leapt to the front of the queue. Kate had been frustrated in her intentions to get an early meeting with Ratcliffe, he would not be in today, it would have to wait. At least it gave her some more time, but to do what?

'First let me apologise. I know you are all doing exceptional work in our operation against grooming gangs and I also share your frustration at the stop, start challenges we are experiencing. I am sure you all want to update me on your findings, but unless you have an almighty revelation it is going to have to take a back seat for a day or two. Is everybody okay with that?' As there was no resistance to Kate's message she turned to DI Kruse.

'Would you like to bring these guys up to speed with our nocturnal visit to Parklands Trent?'

'Yes. Thanks. I'm going to make this short. Myself and DI Taylor staked out a unit on the industrial estate. Having followed leads resulting from the discovery of a body in the river we eventually located a unit in Stanton Road which we believed may have links to the murdered man. We observed over thirty cars coming and going and on a closer inspection by myself I witnessed money being exchanged for entrance to the unit. I also caught sight of a gun on the person of a man who appeared to be acting as some sort of security. We saw no women entering or leaving, only men. Our joint belief is that this is likely to be an illegal prostitution racket. We intend to seek permission for a raid.'

Damian raised his hand but before he could ask his question the phone rang.

'One day I will actually finish a meeting' said Kate. She lifted the receiver and almost immediately a deep frown spread across her face. 'Be right there. Another body has been found in the river, a young girl. DS Kendall and DI Kruse will come with me. DS Rashi you are in temporary control of our investigation into the kebab shop. DC Campbell you are our anchor. Stay here collate all incoming information for both investigations. Everything goes to Tess for compiling. We reconvene at fourteen hundred hours.'

The body had been found much closer to the cement factory, caught in the overhanging branches of a willow tree bending majestically to the water. Helen met the trio of officers.

'By the rivers of Babylon we sat down and wept.' Helen was in a clearly sad, poetic mood, but her words merely puzzled her colleagues. Seeing their failure to understand the allusion she explained.

'The Lament of the Willow? Never mind the poor girl is over there under that tree.' The group walked the short distance to where the pathetic figure of a girl, possibly in her teens, lay entangled in low lying branches, the rivers waters washing by. Incongruously several swifts twittered joyously, their sooty brown feathers showing black in the trees. Her dress was tattered and torn, dark stains hiding any pattern that might be there. Her face was distorted bruised and swollen, one arm resting at an unnerving angle.

Clearly it would be some time before the body was removed and a forensic investigation possible.

'Helen we have a real situation here. We need to move fast. It is our belief that there is a criminal operation involving the prostitution of young girls not far from here. I need to get authorisation for a raid and quickly because if this girl was in any way involved her minders are ruthless, more innocents may suffer and I,' Kate became conscious of the mood of her fellow officers. 'We, have to bring the bastards down, but first we need Ratcliffe to back us and that means evidence.'

Helen was clearly upset, unusual for a seasoned forensic expert used to the trauma of death. 'I'll have enough for you by mid afternoon to ensure you have the wrath of God behind you, let alone the Detective Chief Superintendent

'Thanks Helen I knew we could rely on you.'

Kate and her team trudged back to their car in silence. 'Eve it might be an idea if we take you to have a quick look at the suspected "den", it might help, if we get to be included in the raid, for you to have some idea of the layout because it will be dark if and when we go in.'

'Thanks Kate that would be good.'

They made several discreet passes of the area which compared to the previous night was as quiet as a village church. Once all three were happy with their understanding of the set up they made their way to the office to await the initial forensic report, a wait that would feel like an eternity.

16. Never Enough

The expression on the face of DCS Ratcliffe was difficult to read, the drumming of his fingers on his desk smacked of irritation rather than decision. Small beads of perspiration on his forehead suggested pressure and Kate was well aware, she was the cause of it.

'It's not much DI Taylor.'

Kate looked at him in disbelief. 'Not bloody much Sir. Two killings, one of them a young girl who probably died alone and terrified, abused by who knows how many bastards. Men wearing guns, money passing hands to enter a semi derelict industrial unit. Cars full of dirty old sods, driving around an area deserted by day, that Sir is too bloody much Sir.'

'Calm down DI Taylor.' The tone of Kate's commanding officer's words was stern but understanding. 'At the moment it's circumstantial and the cost of what you are proposing isn't something to be agreed without incredibly careful consideration.'

'Sir another young girl could die while we wait. For absolute certain there are an unknown number of girls being abused both sexually and physically. Sir we are dealing with monsters who have no regard for human life. With respect Sir, sod the money.'

'Normally Kate I would ask for more.' Kate glared. 'However, these pictures of the latest killing together with your deep passion have, against my better judgement, steered me to agree with you. I have already requested information on the availability of a senior firearms team and have been told we could go tonight. You and I have another thirty or so minutes to confirm.'

'Just do it Sir.' Kate surprised herself with her over assertive tone whilst her boss raised his eyebrows in admonition, before allowing himself a rare smile.

'For you Kate.'

'For the girls Sir.'

Kate was recalled to the DCS's office an hour later. 'It's on DI Taylor. In one hour, you will meet with the SO team and give them a full briefing. After that you're out. You and your team get back to your proper assignment. I thank you for your work on this case and you will receive the appropriate recognition internally.'

Kate flared. 'Hold on a minute Sir. There's no way we are being left out of this one Sir. My team have worked bloody hard to get this far and they deserve, no they damn well need to see it through.' Kate could feel her temperature rising, her head was throbbing, she knew both had to stop, she had to stay in control, or she would blow any chance of her guys being there at the "kill".

Ratcliffe chose his words carefully. He had come to have a healthy respect for Kate's determination, but at the same time she had been told the rules when this all started. She had to understand that if her team was to be successful in exposing grooming gangs and for that matter any other horrendous abuses of young girls they had to have a large degree of anonymity. Bursting in on an east European trafficking and prostitution operation wasn't going to do that.

'DI Taylor how many more times do I have to explain?'

'Sir I get it and you're right, when we signed up, we agreed to stay in the background, no fame, no credit. That's fine, but we just need to be there, in the background. Sir it's good for motivation and you must know yourself Sir, it brings closure.'

Ratcliffe emitted a deep sigh. He understood everything Kate was saying. He would be delivering the same passionate speech if their positions were swapped. Something had to give. He reluctantly accepted it would be him, but he wouldn't go all the way, that would be bad form.

'Okay Kate.' Ratcliffe watched DI Taylor's face light up. He was going to take a small amount of satisfaction, both in agreeing in part to her request, but also in the element of denial that accompanied it. 'You and one other can act as observers on the "raid". The rest stay at home.'

Kate instinctively sought to continue the argument, she was winning, she could do this. She raised her head ready for a further round of negotiation but as her eyes met those of the Chief, she changed her mind. This was no time for double or quits, time to take the result and move on.

'Thank you Sir. This will mean a great deal to us Sir, although the rest of my team are going to feel extremely disappointed.'

'If they didn't want to continually face disappointment then they shouldn't have joined the bloody police force should they Kate.'

She smiled for what seemed like the first time that day. 'No Sir, that's for sure.'

Kate would have to explain the situation to her officers and then again would she. It wouldn't be the first time DI Taylor had found a way round an operational instruction she didn't like. Kate determined not to fully communicate Ratcliffe's decision to her team. In fact, she had already decided to leave out the important bit about only two of them attending. She wouldn't disobey Ratcliffe, but she would put back up plans in place.

Eve would accompany her while Rashi, Damian and Tess had been ordered to take up a position just under a mile away. She had explained to them that they were required to block a potential escape route, but that on her command and only on her command, they were to approach the raid site immediately. She would not of course be making such a call, but at least her three colleagues would be under the impression they were part of the action. In Kate's mind this solution kept everybody happy.

It was a particularly dark evening not improved by a smattering of rain that always made such situations less enjoyable, whilst at the same time adding a certain something to the atmosphere of the occasion. Kate had finished briefing DS Kamani, DC Lewis and Campbell and watched as they drove off to take their place on the upcoming stage. She now approached DS Kendall who as usual looked like she was ready for a night at the local, calm, unconcerned, focused.

Kate explained their role again, after all, wasn't repetition supposed to be the breakfast of champions. She cringed. She wasn't ever going to say that to Eve it sounded so crass, a real credibility blower if ever there was one. As far as she was concerned, those sorts of senseless statements should only be mouthed in training sessions.

'We are basically bringing up the rear. It is important we are not seen, our identities need to remain undisclosed if we are to continue our day job. We are here to see closure of a fantastic team effort. We are here to see some ugly bastards being taken down, knowing it's because of us. Having said that if any action comes our way, get stuck in.'

And then in walked DI Kruse, the forgotten man. 'Bugger' muttered Kate. Eve pulled a face and sat down in the corner.

'So, DI Taylor, were you going to tell me about the sortie? And the meeting with Ratcliffe, wasn't I supposed to be there?'

Kate's heart was pounding, this was difficult, she was thinking on her feet and failing to find an answer. Then it came. 'Sorry Trent I thought you knew, the Chief didn't want us on the operation.'

'But apparently you are Kate.'

'Only after a damn hard fight. What did he say to you?' That was the master stroke, the power shifter, the counterattack with bells on.

'He hasn't said anything to me.' DI Kruse looked confused, less confident in his position.

'Well if I were you, I would be banging on his door demanding to go with us.'

Trent Kruse was certain he had been stitched up here, but there was only one thing he could do. With a shake of the head he stormed out the door intent on confronting Ratcliffe.

'That was a bit sneaky Kate. Worked though.' Eve was impressed and offered her boss a high five.

'I know. I was hoping to escape before I saw him, but at the end of the day he's not really one of the team. He's been helpful and good to work with but "Band of Brothers" and all that. Now let's get out of here.

Several vehicles were already leaving the compound bursting at the seams with solid, hard looking men and women, armed to the teeth. Kate almost felt sorry for the people about to receive them, these guys were total professionals, legal hitmen.

Kate and her colleagues had been issued with Glock 17 pistols, light and comfortable, accurate and reliable. The two women appeared casually comfortable with the weapons. Eve took a few moments to reacquaint herself with the feel of it. First in her hand and then in its holster. She slid it in and out several times before clasping it in her palm, fingers caressing the trigger, before raising her arm upwards and to both sides, finally placing it carefully away.

'Let's go. DS Kendall you drive.' Eve was going to anyway, she was in her element, this was by far the best part of being a copper, the time when the good guy sends the bad guy to hell, or at least prison for a long time. They swept out the gates in gentle pursuit of their colleagues and caught up with them a couple of miles down the road keeping a discreet hundred metres behind the convoy ahead. Kate turned on the radio. The voice of Sting singing "I'll be watching you" came on the airwaves.

'Well that's appropriate' said Eve as she gave her own version of the song, restricted to the one line she knew and therefore ending rather quickly much to Kate's relief.

Driving through the estate they could see police vehicles had already taken up positions in all areas of Parklands. Waiting in side roads to intercept incoming traffic, and close to the target sealing off potential exits. They wouldn't be noticed until they wanted to be.

Meanwhile just over a kilometre further down a dark and wet, treelined road leading from the industrial park, their colleagues tried to make themselves comfortable. 'Do you think we'll see any real action tonight Damian?' Tess was eager to experience a "bust" of the size this operation was likely to be. The armed groups of officers had fired her blood. They were a stirring sight, menacing and comforting at the same time. Dead sexy.

'To be honest it's likely to pass us by. Our only real hope of involvement is somebody trying to escape the trap down this road and as you know, if that happens, we don't attempt to apprehend, we just follow. On the other hand, if things get tasty upstream you never know we might be called in to add a bit of muscle.' Damian posed Tarzan like. Tess mockingly squeezed his biceps.

'Ooh you are a big boy.' She laughed outrageously and slid down into her seat ready for a long night.

DI Kamani sat in the back. He was feeling rather more serious. As senior officer he knew all three of their lives were literally in his hands. 'Listen guys, banter's good but remember something very important, it might save your lives. We do not have weapons. Anybody coming down that road most likely will. Be smart, stay alive.'

With that, the humour left the "room".

17. Crow's Nest

Cars were being stopped. Nothing was getting through and those that were already on the estate, weren't getting out. The first part of the operation was going smoothly the net was about to close.

Figures moved rapidly, dark and menacing, focused and composed. The distance to the target was swallowed up, teams moving in different directions, like clockwork. Kate and Eve followed obediently at the tail of such a team. They had been dared to get involved by a huge mountain of a man. They wouldn't disobey him.

A group of five men stood chatting idly outside the Star Enterprise unit. Five cars lined the dust road. The airways crackled, a signal given, the final moves commenced.

Without warning the night air resounded to commands. 'Police. Get down. On the floor.' Shots rang out first one way and then the other. Five men lay on the floor, two of them bleeding profusely, a result they both could, and should have avoided. Within seconds the other three were handcuffed, already on their way from the scene. The entrance had been breached and from the sound of it a similar piece of violent theatre was being played out at the rear of the building.

Half of the officers in Kate's squad had already breezed through the front door, she and Eve ordered to remain outside, ordered to act, and no more, as cover for their colleagues.

Inside elite officers probed, moved forward, first one wave and then the next, an overlapping formation trained to perfection. Against them a disorientated foe. Some stood their ground, groups of two and three. Inevitably one had to go down before the others brought a halt to their pointless resistance. Young girls hugged and cried, behind and under tables, bore witness to the violence, felt the fear.

Those that didn't "stand" ran blindly for cover, desperately seeking a way out of the building. One took a hostage and then a bullet, the girl once imprisoned in his sweating arms now screaming wildly, a heap on the floor, a man's blood smearing her face.

Another burst through a window into the open air, his freedom short, his capture inevitable.

DI Kruse was breathing hard. The adrenalin was pumping, the heat inside the protective gear oppressive and tiring. Shots could be heard but their direction was only made apparent by the whistle of a near miss or the clatter and clang of a ricochet. A few minutes ago he had been scared, a few minutes ago he had considered himself a fool for the demands he had made on his boss. Now he was buzzing. Even in all this action, even through the blur, he had time to smile to himself. 'DI Taylor would be bloody annoyed if she could see him, serves her right.' A figure suddenly appeared in front of him, disturbing his thoughts a little too late. Trent Kruse had allowed himself to be distracted. A shot rang out the man fell, a shadow moved on. Trent breathed a sigh of relief. A second shot rang out. Di Kruse felt a warm sensation slowly meandering through his veins. It suddenly became more rapid and a stain appeared on his trouser leg. His strength drained, his balance disappeared, he slumped to the floor. A black veil dropped over his eyes and for Trent the world returned to silence.

Kate listened to the cacophony of a police bust emanating from the walls of the industrial unit. She had been on several such operations and they all played the same tune. She could tell by the rate of fire, the banging of doors and smashing of windows what stage the action had reached. She raised her phone and called in the rest of her team.

Within minutes Rashi, Tess and Damian had arrived, skirting around the police vans that had arrived hot on the trail of the lead cars. Kate greeted them. 'Hi guys I thought you'd like to be here for the finale. Keep low, watch, listen and learn.'

The new arrivals clustered behind their boss watching and listening the adrenalin pumping. Suddenly everything went quiet, figures began to emerge from the under siege building. Five bodies were dragged from the swirling mist that hung in the air recently released by smoke grenades. Two began to move, both sitting up coughing and swearing, three more lay still. Medics claimed the men for their own and departed, the scene sirens blaring. More officers piled out of the front door, whilst others returned from the rear of the building, their senior officers reporting to command.

Kate moved over to gain some feedback and reached the control group in time to hear part of the initial debrief. 'Four injuries, two with gunshot, one critical.'

'And the suspects?'

'We've counted ten so far. Six dead. There's a possibility of two or maybe three escapees.'

'Rescued?'

'Latest score is twenty nine Sir.'

'Okay get the forensic team in we'll need their report for the inevitable inquiry Good work everybody.'

It had been a long haul but a much needed result. Kate and her team stood grouped together around her car, exhausted, proud, defiant. None of them spoke until suddenly Damian began to smile. It was a reflex action demonstrating how much each one of them had put into this exercise. It could just have easily involved another one of his tears which might have been embarrassing but totally understandable. Damian's icebreaking action saw an almost instantaneous chain reaction as lips broke, heads nodded, fists punched the air. The relief was immeasurable, the feeling that came with success, priceless.

Strangely no words had been spoken, Kate opened her car door and sagging down into the front seat and looking up at them said what they were all thinking. 'You beauties, you incredible bloody amazing bunch of top rank professionals, you will never know what you guys have achieved today, but thank you, thank you so very bloody much for not just today but for your dedication, rugged determination and total belief in what you are doing. That's the first bunch of assholes behind bars, tomorrow we go get some more.'

Her speech drew a further round of adrenalin fuelled celebration. It was going to take some time before any of them wound down. Around them however the machine was clicking into action as ambulances, site preservation teams and forensics experts arrived. People had died, an investigation into how would have to take place. It could never be just a case of the good guys shooting the bad guys, absurdly, but rightly, it had to be done correctly.

Rashi looked like he was about to make his inevitable contribution to Kate's motivational speech but before he could do so three constables led by a serious looking officer strode toward them. His large nose made him appear slightly odd as it dominated his thin face, but it was his eyes that drew your attention in. They were set hard, emotionless, accentuated by high cheek bones and a cropped head, everything pale except his eyes which were too dark. 'Get ready for some praise people' Damian smiled generously in the newcomers' direction awaiting congratulations from their colleagues.

He stopped along with his entourage ten metres from Kate's

car and beckoned her over. 'Detective Inspector Taylor?' Kate nodded. 'I am Detective Inspector Nigel Ramsay and I have the misfortune to tell you I am here to arrest Detective Sergeant Eve Kendal on a charge of murder.' Kate couldn't stop her involuntary turn of the head to stare at Eve who stared back inquisitively.

'You can't be serious, who sent you, this can't be right.' Kate couldn't focus properly her mind was whirling, Eve a murderer?' And then it was clear, a mistake had been made. 'Leave this with me DI Ramsay. There's obviously an error. DS Kendall and I will meet you back at the station and we'll soon sort it out.'

'Sorry DI Taylor, no can do. I have my orders, I don't like it any more than you do, but you know I have to comply.'

Kate's shoulders slumped as the four men swept past her.

'Detective Sergeant Eve Kendall I am arresting you on suspicion of the murder of one Nicholas Kennedy.' He turned to one of his constables 'Please read her rights.'

DI Ramsay placed handcuffs on Eve's wrists and began to lead her away to the awaiting cars. She remained unmoved, almost uncaring, making no effort to resist. Inside she was finding it all a bit surreal. They had investigated, unearthed, and destroyed a prostitution racket releasing scores of young women from the monstrous hands of some east European assholes and here she was being arrested for murder. She laughed realising this probably looked a bit demonic. Never mind whatever this was all about, it certainly had nothing to do with her.

'I'll be right behind you Eve, I'll see you at the station, I will put a stop to this ridiculous charade. Don't worry.' Kate's last words lacked conviction as doubt began its cruel work. Kate looked at the three remaining officers. How could such euphoria turn so quickly to despair, where did this nightmare come from, could Eve really be guilty of murder?

You lot go home, get some well-earned rest, hug your friends and family, be in the office tomorrow, early.' With that she jumped into her car and tore off after Eve.

Halfway to the station Kate realised her pursuit was point-less. She wouldn't be allowed to see Eve until she had been pro-cessed and been subjected to an initial interview. Better to get home have whatever sleep she could manage and support her friend properly in the morning. But first she would take a long hot shower to wash away the filth she felt pervading every pore of her body. Eve wasn't the only one needing her help. What they had all been a part of tonight was going to be ingrained in their souls for some time. Her team might be buoyant now but sooner or later one or all of them would need some emotional back up.

18. Surely Not?

Eve sat drumming her fingers on the well-worn table, in a room she knew so well. Sparse in appearance, four black plastic chairs to accompany the table, a tape recorder. Normally she was sat on the other side, normally she would be asking the questions. It would be different this time. Two officers would enter eventually and sit opposite her. A gaggle more would congregate behind the one way mirror. She realised for the first time why so many suspects interred in this room ended up giving 'V' signs in the direction of that glass.

Meanwhile a posse of her fellow officers gathered to discuss the evidence and the approach they would be taking with an experienced police officer, a suspect who knew all the tricks and was well known for using every single one of them to excellent effect. Kate was not present. As her team leader she could have no part to play. Instead DI Ramsay would be at the helm. Addressing the three other officers in the room he began to outline procedure.

'DS Caulker and myself will join DS Kendall in the interrogation room. You two will observe and ensure the interview is recording and filming. You will make notes on your observations of the behaviour of the suspect.'

'Is she really a suspect Sir? That's DS Kendall in there Sir.'

'Of course she's a suspect, and make sure you don't forget that fact DS Caulker. After all we have the murder weapon in our possession, it has her finger prints all over it. So yes, she is very much a suspect. Come on let's get this over with.'

Eve had been prepared for a long wait. She knew the score and so she was pleasantly surprised when the door to the interview room opened and in walked her would be "assassins". She admonished herself. These guys were just doing their job. This was only the beginning and anyway she had nothing to hide. Clearly something had happened for her to be here, but it would be no problem at all for her to explain away any connection they might think she had with any murder. She would stop off at the Kings and enjoy a nice pint, maybe a large brandy before bed.

DI Ramsay went through the preliminaries about who was present and grandly announced the tape recording had commenced. She remembered how many times she had done the same and hoped beyond hope she had not sounded so bloody stupid.

'DS Kendall you stand charged with the murder of James Hewitt of Loxborough Yorkshire on the night of 23rd May. Do you understand?'

Eve looked at the Detective Inspector. She wanted to laugh inappropriate as it would be. The serious look on the face of DI Ramsay somehow made it worse. Nothing about his features matched, large nose slightly squinty but also steely eyes, cropped hair. What was he, thug, or wily inquisitor? 'Yes' she finally replied.

'Where were you on that night DI Kendall?' Of all the nights Eve had spent working or in the pub, on reflection, this particular night she had been at home, a warm bath, an early night, no witnesses. She related the fact to the man across the table.

'Out of respect to you DI Kendall I am going to get straight to the point.'

'Good' replied Eve. 'I would like to be clocking off.'

'I'm afraid that isn't going to happen.' Ramsay sounded genuine. He placed a carefully bagged knife on the table. 'The suspect has been shown the murder victim a fifteen centimetre knife.' Blood stained the blade.

Eve smiled at Ramsay what else was she supposed to do.

'The knife has your finger prints on the handle DI Kendall.'

Eve froze. Her smile turned sour. Had she heard correctly, her fingerprints, impossible. The truth dawned, she was indeed in the proverbial. How stupid can you get? 'I guess I'll be needing a solicitor.' Eve slumped back in her chair. The interview was over.

19. Crow Food

She always woke up tired. Her stomach was cramping, her breathing shallow. She slipped her feet from beneath the sheets and swayed as she sat herself up, feet dangling from the bed. She took a few moments to compose herself, rub the sleep from her eyes, partially clear her befuddled brain.

The house was quiet. School today? Unlikely. Food? No appetite. Life? No energy.

Layla Coyle would have had a plan if she could focus, a way forward if she cared, but on one else did, so it was simple. Take care of number one.

Her mother wasn't home, she rarely was first thing in the morning. When she finally arrived, she either slept or sat in front of the telly, glass in hand.

Sometimes Layla would want it all to stop but once she was amongst her friends it wasn't so bad. She did however need some help. Why hadn't the coppers listened? She could have escaped then. She needed help. Where could she find more girls? She and Mel were having to do it all themselves. She needed help. She could stop. That's what she should do, her and Mel just stop. Where was Mel, she would find her, go to the café have some fun.

Layla spasmed, before rushing to the toilet. A sprinkle of water, a token brush of the teeth, hands drawn quickly through her hair. A phone call to Mel. A meeting arranged.

The two girls sat with fizzing drinks going flat in a small back street breakfast bar. A piece of toast had been shared, half eaten. Two hours had passed. They knew the girls were there. They were always there. They would call.

Mel had been a good friend for a long time, or so it seemed, Layla wasn't sure. She looked at the girl across the table and wondered if she was looking in a mirror. Mel was thin, dark eyes, dark shadows. Her brownish hair lay on her face, a face made pale by a lack of everything. She and Layla were of a similar height, same young age. They should be pitied, they were avoided, scorned.

'Better do school tomorrow.' These were the first words spoken for some time. It didn't matter who they came from because they were not a reference for today.

Layla's phone rang. 'Is that them?'

'No it's just my mum.'

'Are you gonna answer?'

Layla stared at the phone on the table and let it play out its tinny tune. 'No.'

It was another hour before the mobile rang again. Once more Mel looked up expectantly. Layla nodded into the phone. 'We're wanted.' The girls left.

The woman recoiled in horror. She ran wildly through the alley the scene she had witnessed rampaging through her mind. She still smelt the depravity, saw the snarls, felt the disdain, as she stumbled into the main road escaping the clutches of the narrow aisle from which she fled.

She looked back down the passageway. She had not been followed. She had merely interrupted their "fun", they would continue, they were untouchable.

'Kate there's a woman at the desk, seems pretty shaken up, she's mumbling about a girl and two men, wants to speak to a woman cop as she puts it. Can you come and talk to her?' Bill Carter glanced across at the middle aged woman sitting apprehensively in the corner. She was clasping her hands together wringing them, deep in thought.

'Be right there Sarge. Would you take her to an interview room please. Number two is the least uncomfortable, get the front desk covered and stay with her until I get there.'

'Yes Ma'am, I'll get some tea and biscuits sorted out as well.'

Kate immediately made her way to Interview room number two. She thanked the Sergeant and sat down opposite a deeply troubled woman, her tea spilling into its saucer as her hands trembled. Kate waited, giving the woman a chance to settle into her new surroundings. Police stations weren't the most hospitable of places at the best of times. They certainly weren't suited for people on the verge of a breakdown, well at least not innocent ones.

'Take your time madam there's no hurry to talk to me. Begin when you are ready. DI Taylor took a drink from her own mug watching closely as the other person in the room slowly recovered her composure and looking up began to speak.

'I heard it was going on, but I didn't expect it to be just happening on the street. You've got to stop it officer its vile, its degrading it's got be stopped.'

'Please calm down.' Kate searched the contact form Sergeant Carter had left behind for her. 'Mrs Lansdowne isn't it?'

'Yes Jill, please call me Jill.'

'My name is Detective Inspector, Kate Taylor. Jill, you've obviously had a terrible shock, witnessed a distressing incident. Perhaps it would be easier if I asked some questions and guided us through this. Would that be okay?'

Mrs Lansdowne nodded. Kate opened the notebook strategically placed to be ready for this moment. Referring to it too soon in these circumstances could be detrimental to the process. 'In your own words Jill, what did you see? Take a deep breath and just summarise the events.'

'I was taking a shortcut behind St Anne's Road.' Kate looked up fleetingly before making a note. 'Two men were standing against a wall. At first I didn't notice the girl on her knees. They just stared at me, their teeth were.... that poor girl, it was disgusting Inspector.'

Kate's attention had been fully engaged. 'Jill you said St Anne's Road. Is that the one in Roche?'

Jill nodded. 'Yes the lane behind the shops, locals use it to get to Aldi's.'

'A lane?' How had they missed the lane?

'Yes.'

'Have you ever witnessed anything at all similar, or even groups of young women or men there before?' Kate spoke in a compassionate tone hiding her desperate need to know more.

'There have been occasions when small groups of girls have been messing about and at times they have been a bit rowdy, a bit disrespectful, but this girl she was being abused by two much older men.'

'Jill think hard before answering this. Please describe the girl.'

'She was thin, dirty shoulder length hair, jeans I think, a red top. She was young perhaps fifteen.'

'Good Jill. And the men?'

'Overweight, grubby, short hair, one of them had bad teeth.' Kate recognised the pattern of fixation on a particular detail, in this case bad teeth. 'Asian, or maybe Turkish, I mean there is a kebab shop out front.'

The last observation was typical, but Kate could not correct it's random thread. 'Mrs Lansdowne thank you so much for reporting this. I am so sorry you have had to experience what must have been a simply awful ordeal. Clearly the poor girl was undergoing an even worse experience and without the help of people like yourself the perpetrators of such vile acts would never be brought to justice. Now, I'm going to ask you to do one thing for me and it isn't going to be easy. Please do not mention this to anyone else.' Jill Lansdowne stared blankly at Kate. 'We are already investigating certain situations the details of which I cannot at this moment disclose to you. If we were to charge in and look for these men now we would be showing our hand too early. This would risk other men, like those you saw, escaping justice. I am sure you wouldn't want that to happen would you Jill?'

Mrs Lansdowne shook her head. 'You can count on my silence Detective but don't let that girl down. From what I've heard too many people are turning a blind eye and I just hope you are not one of those people.' Jill had regained some of her composure and there was just a glint of a threat in her words.

'No Jill I can assure you I am not. I will see this through believe me. Thank you for your help. Would you be so kind as to give my Sergeant a written account of what happened, and I will get to work to find and punish those men. Please wait here, Sergeant Carter won't be long, and once again thank you.'

Kate instructed Bill Carter and returned to her office. There was something going on in Roche, she knew it and now she had the first strands of proof.

20. Ruffling Feathers

'Did you hear about DI Kruse Ma'am?'

Kate's team had been waiting patiently for her. It seemed like a lifetime ago that they had witnessed the bringing down of a prostitution racket and the freeing of so many poor girls. It seemed even longer ago they had been working on their true operation and they were all now eager to focus on their task.

'DI Kruse? What do you mean Rashi?

'He was one of the casualties during the raid Ma'am. I thought you would have heard.'

Kate's mind was racing it seemed like she hadn't had a moment to think for the last forty eight hours, but surely she should have known, and how the hell did Trent Kruse become a "casualty".

'They operated on him and he's in a critical condition, but they seem to think he is going to pull through. Lost a boat load of blood apparently.'

It still wasn't registering. Kate couldn't reconcile the fact he was actually there, let alone how he came to be in the thick of the action. She promised herself she would get to the hospital as soon as she could but in the meantime, he was unfortunately not the priority.

'Right back to basics. Thanks for your patience this morning.

We've had a massive breakthrough.' Kate let the information sink in. 'I have been interviewing a woman who claims to have seen a young girl performing a sex act on a middle aged man. Guess where.'

Kate realised what she had said and just hoped nobody decided to make the obvious remarks. Before they could she completed her report. 'Behind the kebab shop. There were two of them and according to the witness they showed absolutely no respect for either her or the girl.'

'So what's the plan Ma'am.' Damian spoke the words with an edge felt no doubt by everyone in the room.

'I think you know what I am going to say. It's not enough.' Everyone in the force hated those words. They seemed to be created by people who were too lazy to get off their chair and make something happen, happy to sit there until every "I" was dotted, every "T" crossed and all they had to do was turn up and take the credit for a bust that should have been made six months earlier.

'So, what's the plan Ma'am?' Damian repeated his question. Kate was about to give him a mouthful for his attitude but quickly realised it was the right one for the occasion.

'You just lost one more" life" DC Lewis. Make sure it's the last one you lose.

Damian appreciated his lucky escape and determined to clamp up for a while.

'Ma'am.' Rashi spoke next although his approach was determined by the exchange that had just taken place. 'DI Kendall Ma'am?'

Kate felt trapped, the walls closing in, her head throbbing, neck muscles tightening, Her mouth dry. She wanted to scream. Recent events had finally caught up with her and there was only one way out. 'Eve's is going to be fine, she's a big girl and she wouldn't want us concerning ourselves over a little matter like a murder charge, so let's put that aside for now. In the meantime, sod the lot of them. We are going freaking pervert hunting.'

This was about as much loss of control her team or anyone else had ever or were likely witness and the shock was apparent throughout the room. 'Ma'am' queried Rashi.

'I'll rephrase that. We are going to do our job and where people are preying on innocent girls, or boys for that matter, we are going to put them behind bars, and it starts, at the kebab shop.' Kate explained her interview with Mrs Lansdowne. 'So, this afternoon, same time of day as our witness' claims she saw the indecency taking place, Tess, you will take a walk through the back lane at regular intervals. The rest of us will be stationed at both entrances which looking at the map are not visible from the rear of the shop. As soon as you see something you should radio us, but make sure you keep eyes on the incident. We must catch them in the act. Any questions? No? Good. We go in two hours.'

DI Taylor was angry with herself. Trent Kruse was fighting for his life and she hadn't known, Eve Kendall was fighting for her career and her freedom and she had forgotten all about her, albeit only for a short time. She had two visits to make before kick-off.

Kate had been unable to see either of her colleagues. It seemed rules always started with the word "No." She had to put them from her mind. That's how it worked. Tess had made several unremarkable trips up and down the lane. Kate decided to stretch her legs and together they made another venture into the alleyways behind the main street. They turned a sharp bend in the lane framed by tall red brick buildings and there they were. One man his trousers around his ankles stared at the sky as a small thin figure knelt before him. Another had backed similarly sized female up against a wall and was rocking vigorously, guttural sounds emanating from his frenzied form. Kate felt sick but before she could radio the boys in, Tess launched herself at the nearest form knocking him sideways. As she clambered over his fat clammy body handcuffs in hand, the second man recovered his wits and made an aggressive move toward her. His attempt failed in a style which would have been considered funny under different circumstances. For whatever reason he had overlooked the fact his trousers were impeding his legs, and in his haste, he merely tumbled headlong to the floor.

Kate pounced. 'You're nicked sunshine.' Tess already had her man under control, sitting uncomfortable against the wall hands restrained. She was busy calling in Rashi and Damian who appeared seconds later when neither of them could help but smile at their friends.

'Stop grinning like chipmunks. 'You two take over. Do the necessaries and we'll have a nice little chat with these two gentlemen back at the station. DC Campbell with me, let's see if we can catch those girls. They set off down the alley in the same direction as the girls had fled as soon as Tess flattened her target. They had a good start on the officers and their search was inevitably fruitless. Walking back to the crime scene Kate confronted Tess over her actions.

'What was that all about DC Campbell?'

'Sorry Ma'am I just couldn't help myself. Those disgusting blokes, I just lost it.'

'I totally understand DC Campbell, but you have to learn to take time to think. What if they had been armed? What if they were in a compromising but innocent situation with "friends". What if they had overpowered us and disappeared? What if you had injured one of them and then our case collapsed through lack of evidence?'

Tess looked abashed. 'Sorry Ma'am.'

'It's done now DC Campbell, but make sure you learn from it or else you will have wasted the experience and becoming a good copper is all about experience. Let's go and ask some difficult questions.'

21. Both Sides

The recording was running. Four figures sat around a cheap table in a stark room. Remarkably all four were confident. The preliminaries had been completed. The gloves were off, the challenge accepted.

DI Kendall I won't beat about the bush.' He placed the plastic bag containing the nasty looking knife in front of Eve Kendall. It was a grim weapon both for its length and the obvious blood stains decorating its blade. 'I'll ask you again. Have you seen this weapon before?'

Eve took a cursory glance at the item before her. 'Yes.' She replied with a very deep sigh.

The two officers on the other side of the table looked surprised, almost shocked. 'Is it your knife DI Kendall?'

'No.'

'So where have you seen it before?'

'In a pub.' Eve's answers were short and sparse, she was too busy thinking, to turn a phrase, too concerned about what she would be saying. She was already three or four questions ahead of her interrogators and she didn't like the scenario she was considering.

'Come on Eve.' DI Ramsay was not happy playing games. He knew he was in a battle of wits and he wasn't enjoying it particularly. 'Which pub? When? Under what circumstances did you see the knife?

'The Kings Arms, a few weeks ago, a man I know as Terry Frost asked me to take it away from him.' Eve cringed inwardly. Her tale was so bloody weak, true, but believable? She wasn't sure.

'And did you take the blade away from him?'

'No.'

DI Ramsay's exasperation was mounting. 'DI Kendall the knife you have identified was used to kill a man and as I have previously informed you, it has your finger prints on it.'

'Eve knew why. She had scanned her memory, viewing in her mind in some detail, the night she met Terry Frost.

'Where were you on the night of 23rd May DS Kendall?'

'Last Saturday? I'm pretty sure I have already told you I was at home, I had a thumping headache, an early night, left the pub after the afternoon football, and before you ask, no witnesses to the home bit.'

For the first time eve's solicitor spoke. 'I would like to stop this interview to enable me to discuss the points that have been raised so far. Shall we say two hours.'

'Agreed.' DS Holden brought the recording to an end and the officers left the room.

'I am sure you have a prefect explanation Eve and I would really like to hear it.'

Eve relayed her story of how she had met Terry Frost in her local pub, how he had tricked her into holding a knife he owned. 'Yes, my finger prints are on the knife and that's because it has been in my hand. No, I don't have an alibi because I was on my own on the night of the murder. But I do have a witness to the meeting with Frost. All the police have to do is interview Harry Allerton the owner of the pub, and Frost. Job done.'

Her solicitor looked at her from under her Armani glasses. Jane Pickford combined intelligence with a beguiling face. Her blue eyes shone inquisitively suggesting more questions than her lips conveyed. 'You make it sound easy Eve. Did your man Harry see you holding the knife?'

'No. I doubt it. But it will be on the pub CCTV.'

'Well that's a start.'

Jane Pickford shifted in her chair and pushed her greying hair back behind both ears. 'And do you think Mr Frost will confess Eve, because strange though it may seem to you, I don't. If he's been smart enough to stitch you up, he will have been just as clever in creating a few more strands to his story. Still let's make a start by getting your friends in blue to bring your two men in for interviews.'

The investigating officers were called back into the room and Jane suggested the two men mentioned by Eve should be interviewed before the proceedings went any further. Both DI Ramsay and his colleague were of a mind to oblige. He felt he had his murderer sat in front of him, but he wasn't happy, she was a copper and it grated.

It felt like he wasn't really there. People were talking, procedures were clearly being followed, his agreement was being sought. He was nodding his head. He couldn't recall why. His solicitor touched his arm. 'Are you okay?'

Terry Frost switched on. 'Yes fine, I'm fine, just want it over with really. It seems so unreal.'

'In your own time Terry. Remember what I said. Think before you answer and if you don't have the answer don't feel obliged to speak.' Terry Frost nodded.

'Mr Frost are you aware this interview is being recorded.' He thought he had been asked that question already, why were they asking again. They seemed concerned. Why? He was feeling hot, sweating. He had to concentrate or the game would be over. 'Yes.'

One of the officers placed a bag on the table. It contained a knife. He had a name. Terry was sure he had been told his name. It didn't matter. 'Is this your knife Mr Frost?'

He peered through the plastic. 'It was.'

'It was. What do you mean Sir?'

'It was my knife, but I gave it away.' The sweating hadn't stopped, his ears were half blocked, his own voice was muffled. He ran his hand through his hair.

'Who did you give it to.'

'Eve Kendall.'

The two investigating officers looked at each other before the one on the right continued.

'Why did you give it to her.'

'I asked her to get rid of it for me. I was angry I thought I might harm someone.'

'And did she "Get rid of it" Mr Frost.'

'I don't know.' This was much harder than he had expected, it wasn't the questions it was more a case of what was behind the questions. They seemed innocent enough but were they designed to trap him. He focused, he was doing alright.

'I've no idea.'

'Where did you give the knife to DS Kendall?'

This was the question he had been waiting for, a chance to elaborate, his previous stiffness to be substituted with innuendo and conceit. 'It was at her local pub, the Kings Arms. I asked the landlord to arrange a meeting. I was distressed, my daughter was missing. I knew I wasn't thinking clearly. I have a temper and this time I had even frightened myself. She helped to calm me down.'

'Why DI Kendall?'

Terry Frost explained the incident at the swimming pool, how he felt confidence in the way Eve Kendall had carried out her duties and because of her past. This was the tie down. He made the statement and awaited the reaction.

'Her past Mr Frost?'

'Everyone knows Eve was abused as a child. She didn't talk about it but if the subject of child abuse came up in a conversation, she would go quiet. A huge anger would be simmering. In some ways it was quite concerning, you know, "if looks could kill and all that".

'Where were you on the night of 23rd May?' It was a final question both officers still holding in their heads the revelation of Eve Kendall's abuse. Perhaps the final nail in her particular coffin.

'At home with my wife. You can check with her.'

'We will Mr Frost. Thank you that will be all for now. You may go, we will be in touch.'

He had done it. Suddenly he felt sick. He needed to think. Terry drove to the Dog and Duck, it would be quiet.

DI Kendall joked freely with her legal representative. It had taken another day but Eve was feeling confident in Harry's testimony. Frost was another matter, but he would slip up sooner or later they always did.

Ramsay and Holden entered the room looking unexpectedly morose. Eve's good mood abated slightly, her training sensing things hadn't quite, gone to plan.

'Di Kendall.' Ramsay spoke quietly, almost apologetically. 'Unfortunately, Harry Allerton cannot confirm your story.'

'You've got to be kidding me.' Eve's voice exploded across the room.

'Let me finish DI Kendall. He is unable to corroborate your version of events because he is in hospital. He had a stroke yesterday afternoon and is currently in a coma.'

'There's still the CCTV.' Jane Pickford looked supportively at Eve as she spoke, 'Have you obtained the footage of the night in question.'

DI Ramsay glanced to the side, his upper lip twitching, composing himself for the next few words he would need to utter. 'The CCTV at the Kings Arms does not cover the whole pub. There are nooks and crannies where tables and chairs cannot be seen. We can confirm the meeting took place as we have evidence of both DI Kendall and Mr Frost entering and leaving but I'm afraid that's it. Taking everything into consideration it doesn't look good.'

22. Scarecrows Can't Move

Kate Taylor sat on the sofa in the ante room waiting for DCS Ratcliffe. His Personal Assistant sat typing, no doubt replying to an invitation to some lavishly funded event for the high and mighty. Kate was amusing herself by trying to decide if she was jealous. Her opinion would be decided by the food. Scallops would sway that decision, a choice of amazing wines would set it in concrete.

Jon Ratcliffe finally entered. He spoke to his PA first. 'Accept the invitation from the Christmas Charity Ball, reject the Braunton Lib Dems, usual wording prior engagements, that sort of thing.' DCS Ratcliffe knew he didn't need to tell his secretary what to say, but old habits died hard.

'With me Kate.' He disappeared into his office without another glance. Kate deliberately took her time, opening her bag and checking its contents before following. DCS Ratcliffe sat, hands clasped across his ever increasing girth. Kate made a mental note not to get promoted. Fine chance.

Ratcliffe's impatience showed. Kate's childish delight at the annoyance she was creating didn't.

'Reports DI Taylor. Bit behind aren't we.' Kate maintained her silence. 'Supposed to be every day.' Ratcliffe sat circling his thumbs. 'Still I suppose there has been rather a lot going on.' He sighed. 'All excellent work.' Kate waited for the "but". She did not have to wait long.

'Excellent work indeed, until yesterday.'

The comment was expected. Kate and her team had opened a can of worms. Arrest a certain type of criminal and await the outrage. Turn a blind eye, everyone's a victim of something. Release the suspects, counsel the abused. Move on. Kate wasn't about to.

'Yesterday Sir?'

DCS Ratcliffe was about to annoy Kate Taylor. His nose twitched. 'Ever since you arrested your suspects, I have had nothing but grief from the Asian Community. My police force is being called a racist organisation, that imbecile of a councillor Saad Hassan is being his usual pain in the ass and the local MP is not behaving much better. And do you know what the real problem is DI Taylor?'

A rhetorical question which Kate steadfastly ignored.

'You bloody well botched it.'

It was time to bring an end to her silence, it had become personal. 'And how Sir, did I botch it Sir?' Her tone was not respectful, it wasn't meant to be. Nobody attacked Kate Taylor without getting a slap back.

'No evidence DI Taylor. Only the word of two police officers and we both know how the press can make that look. Yes, it's a sad day when they can insinuate and slander a copper, but they can, and they do. And guess what Kate, they have. The girls the suspects are supposed to have abused ran away and you DI Taylor are left with nothing. And me? I am left with a bloody great headache.'

Kate had to admit it, if only to herself, she was snookered. Ratcliffe had several very good points. Strangely under the circumstances she was also happy. She had shaken the hornets' nest and they had all come out to sting her. And as far as Kate was concerned, their protests told a story of their own.

'Kate why didn't you wait, build a case, get the main men not some dirty old blokes in a back alley. Really DI Taylor I can't believe you acted so rashly. I was hoping I would be able to expand your team, instead you're lucky I'm not going to close it down. Yet.'

'I hear what you are saying Sir, really I do, but did you expect me to stand by while one girl was getting shagged against a wall and another was having a grubby pervert shove his dick down her throat.'

For a short moment Ratcliffe looked shocked not so much at the outburst as at the words Kate had used. 'Your description of events DI Taylor are at present not matching those of the press or the Community and they will not win the day in court. Witnesses, witnesses, reliable witnesses Kate, that's all I ask, give that to me and I promise you I will take on the world. Without them, well, as you already know I have had to release the two men.'

Kate shrugged. 'You want the men at the top Sir?'

'Yes Kate.'

'Caught in the act Sir?'

'Yes Kate.' His answer carried a degree of caution.

'With witnesses Sir, Reliable witnesses Sir.'

'Careful DI Taylor.'

'Then you shall have them Sir but when I deliver them to you on a plate their balls in their mouths you had damn well better stand up and be counted, Sir.' Kate didn't wait for the explosion, she had no appetite for a further reprimand, the gloves were well and truly off. It was knuckle duster time.

Ratcliffe remained. He relaxed now that it was over. Patricia Jennings entered the office. She was the most important person in Jon Ratcliffe's professional life. She was petite, pretty, so efficient, loyal, happy to pander to his every need.

'Your next appointment is in ten minutes Sir.' Ms Jennings Flicked nonchalantly through a pile of papers resting on her arm before depositing them on the desk. Her perfume filled DCS Ratcliffe's head despite the distance created by the furniture. He was very fond of his PA and so incredibly sad for the tragedy in her life. Losing her son and husband in a car crash was a terrible thing to have to live with.

'Would you like a coffee before DC Campbell arrives.'

'You read my thoughts again Patricia. I'll need one. Please go heavy with the sugar.' They smiled knowingly at each other before Jon Ratcliffe was alone once more.

At first Tess had relished the confidence that had been shown to her. Now as she waited for another meeting she was beginning to feel differently. This would be the third. There had been telephone conversations snatched during the day or late at night, brief and enquiring, warm but unsettling. Too often now the direction of the questioning felt uncomfortable. She assumed this was how it had to be. Only time would tell.

'Go on in DC Campbell he will be here in a minute. Can I get you a tea? Coffee?' DCS Ratcliffe's PA was always kind to Tess. It was appreciated.

'Thanks, and no thanks. Tess placed herself on one of the chairs facing the large wooden desk and waited. Ratcliffe arrived.

'Good to see you DC Campbell. I must say with all the excitement your team have been generating your attachment to it will go a long way to aiding your fast tracking. Tell me, what have you learned?'

Tess had learned one hell of a lot. The problem was there was one large part of it she didn't like, her head was in a spin. Play the game, move upward, or be true to yourself and live with the results. It felt too much like a form of Russian Roulette. Which path should she follow?

'I've certainly realised I have an enormous amount to learn. I also know I have the ability and the strength to achieve everything I want to.' Her last words were throwaways, the inane self-promotion she was expected to spout.

'Which particular event has taught you the most.'

The answer was easy. It was the appalling failure of the establishment to back police officers in their pursuit of the grooming gangs. It was the pathetic crumbling of authority in the face of political necessity.

'Each event has taught me something different. The need for mundane research, the dedicated analysis, the importance of timing or the attention to detail required for an effective raid. All of these things are of equal importance, each stage critical in a positive outcome.' Tess had buckled under the pressure. Her career mattered.

'And what about your colleagues DC Campbell. How are they performing.' That time had arrived, the real reason for her posting, the glue that would cement her onward march up the ladder. Tess sighed and began her report

The car park was quite therapeutic. Kate had arrived early and had decided to compose herself before the trying time ahead. She was completely pissed off by what had happened. Politics and police work don't mix. Unfortunately, she also recognised her own mistakes. They wouldn't happen again. If there was an "again". Kate grinned fretfully before opening the car door and heading to a showdown, long overdue.

Kate ignored DC Campbell as she swept through the main office to her room. Tess followed.

'Ma'am I need to speak to you.'

Kate turned her shoulder and cast her eyes over her DC, a hint of malice lingering in her expression. She rose above it. 'Yes Tess, it might be time.'

'Ma'am I...' Tess began to speak. Kate motioned to her to stop, taking her time to sit down. She was still not sure what position she was going to take with her. She decided to listen, directing her young officer to continue.

'Ma'am I am part of a fast track scheme, as you know. I guess to most of you that means I am a pain in the ass and not to be trusted.' Kate admired this approach, it had promise. 'And you're right Ma'am I shouldn't be trusted.' Kate would have stopped her then but her guilt or was it shame kept her going. 'DCS Ratcliffe as part of my career path asked me to keep regular reports on you and the others. I have been doing that but Ma'am. I can't do it any longer. I've realised my team are more important than getting a helping hand from above. I want to keep working with you and the guys Ma'am, but I will understand if you cannot live with that.'

Kate didn't at this stage want to prolong the agony, but she couldn't help herself. She let DC Campbell stew. 'Please sit down. I commend your courage in telling me this. However, I already knew.'

'You knew but how.'

'You wouldn't be the first high flyer to betray their fellow officers and you won't unfortunately be the last. Unlike you not everyone sees the light.'

'I'm not a Detective Inspector because I'm pretty DC Campbell. And let me tell you now, there's one thing above all else that really puts me in a bad place, and that is when somebody thinks I am stupid, and you DC Campbell clearly did.'

'Ma'am I....' Kate held up a hand to stop her digging a deeper hole.

'Tess there's a way round this. The girls from the prostitution gang raid have slowly been giving up information about the alleged leader of the group. Their initial fear of the other gang members is thinning. From what they are saying and the identification process of both the bodies and the blokes in the cells, the leader escaped and probably his "oppo" with him. Because of the awful condition these girls are in, and the amount of drugs they have been forced to consume during their captivity, we can't be sure how authentic their claims are.

If you have genuinely chosen your side, and assuming it is our side you have chosen, we can set up a situation which might solve your dilemma.'

'Anything Ma'am.'

I am going to ask you to effectively step aside from the team for a while and take a really deep look at whether this guy escaped or not. Interview the girls, recheck any CCTV, talk to the armed officers on the raid, see if forensics have anything, go back to the scene give it a thorough perimeter check. This is important work DC Campbell. If you can prove he is still at large we will go and get him. It also means of course you will have nothing to report on your colleagues because you won't be with them. Make a good job of this and you will get brownie points upstairs whilst me and my team can do our thing without worrying about a knife in the back. Are you on board?'

'Oh yes Ma'am. Yes please Ma'am. Thank you so much Ma'am.'

Kate gave her a withering look. 'Last chance. Now don't let me keep you DC Campbell you have work to do.'

23. Help At Hand

The door shut. There was nothing intimidating about a prison cell if you weren't the one locked inside. It probably was if you were. Kate didn't know.

'Hello Eve.'

'Kate.'

It was an uneasy meeting. Their relationship hadn't received the time it needed, to be considered sound. Two such women, didn't always need time.

'From what I've read you could do with a break.'

Eve laughed. 'Yes I was thinking maybe the Bahamas for a fortnight. Do you think you could arrange that?'

The ice was broken. 'Seriously is there anything I can follow up, and listen Eve, if what I find doesn't help, then I didn't find it.'

'If you or I could get that prick Frost in an interview room I am sure we could very quickly sort it, but that isn't going to happen anytime soon is it. There's only one other avenue I can think of and that's the barmaid Jenny Hargreaves at the Kings Arms. She wasn't there when I met Frost but I'm in the shit, so anything is worth a try. With Harry being out for the count I guess she will be running things full time.'

'I'll go there tonight.' Kate gripped Eve's shoulder and looked her in the eye. No words were necessary. They smiled and Kate

Taylor left.

Kate had commandeered Damian for the trip to the Kings Arms. She could use the evening to get a closer insight into this young man who seemed far too nice to be a copper, but clearly had a slice of steel running through him when it was needed. The pub was quiet, a young woman of average height was polishing the beer taps. She looked tired, shadows stamped under her pale grey eyes. Her long brown hair was in need of a brush, most likely a wash as well.

'Jenny Hargreaves?'

'Who's asking.' The reply was terse, strained unwelcoming.

'No wonder the pub's empty. I've been made more welcome at a National Front meeting.' Damian accompanied his words with a broad smile. Jenny unconsciously ran her fingers through her hair, her eyes showing interest.

'Sorry, I'm a little bit stressed, my boss is in hospital, had a stroke and I'm not really coping.' Her eyes welled, she dragged her tongue across her dry lips, her chin wavered.

'We understand Jenny, we know all about your situation.' Jenny looked surprised. 'I'm DI Kate Taylor and this is DC Lewis. You know our colleague Eve Kendall.'

'Eve? Oh my goodness how is she. It's not true, Eve's is as tough as old boots but no, she didn't murder anyone.'

'We don't think so either Jenny. Eve needed Harry as a witness to a meeting she had with Terry Frost but obviously at the moment Harry can't help. We were hoping we could have a chat, unofficially that is.' Kate stared at Jenny. 'And I mean unofficially at this point.'

Jenny was not sure what the officer meant but was more than happy to help in any way she could. 'I wasn't here till later that night so I didn't see what happened between them.'

'No, we know that but is there anything you can think of no matter how insignificant it might seem to you. Did Harry or Eve mention anything that night or any other night since?'

Jenny thought for a while but there was nothing.

Kate's gaze wandered around the lounge bar recalling the scenes from the CCTV. She had watched every inch and felt she knew the pub inside out. There were three places she could visualise as not having been visible on the recording. The meeting had to have taken place in one of those. Eve's testimony suggested the seats could be seen from the bar. She remembered Eve stating that she saw Frost receive a phone call. That meant there was only one place she could have sat.

'Go and sit over there DC Lewis.' Kate pointed to an alcove, red velvet covering three benches, a round wooden table set between them.

Damian had been listening, but he had to confess he had been more interested in the girl. He was too quick to fall in love or so his mum told him. His musings were interrupted by his DI.

'What do you see Lewis.' Damian's first reaction was to flirt with Jenny, to deliver a throwaway line, "the girl of my dreams" he thought better of it. He concentrated for the first time since he had entered the pub. He considered what he saw through the eyes of a customer and then he put himself behind the bar. He had spent a bit of time working in pubs as a student. He had enjoyed the experience. He liked the atmosphere. The banter, the smells.

'In your own time DC Lewis.'

'How many tills are there Jenny?'

'Two.'

'So there's one by you, and I'm looking straight at the other one right? Are they both always used?' The bar swept around in an "L" shape. Damian could see both tills. He rose and strode toward the nearest one.

'The one you are looking at we normally only use for busy nights.'

'Do you bring in part time staff for the busy nights?'

'Yes we do.'

Damian was focused on the ceiling above the till and then on the mirror and the wall behind it. 'Was Harry a trusting man?'

Kate was standing, elbow on bar, watching with approval as her junior officer plied his trade. Okay he was showing off to the barmaid, that much was obvious, but there was also the first glimpses of a fine, future investigator at large here.

'Don't worry I'll answer that. He wasn't. There's a camera above the till. Old trick to stop dishonest staff from fiddling. Casuals have a tendency to give their friends a bit more change than they should, and the camera covers the till tray. They also give away free drinks and there's a second camera covering the bar, and with any luck, it's view might stretch a bit further. Jenny had sidled around to the second till. 'The sly old bugger. Didn't mention a word of this to me. I can't even see the bloody things.'

Damian joined her behind the bar, getting up close and pointing to the mirrors. 'Take a good look. See those screws in the glass. They're not screws.'

'You clever sod DC Lewis.' Kate slapped Damian on the back.

'Thank you Ma'am, I think.'

'Jenny where would Harry have viewed this camera?'

She took them through a corridor and led them to a room behind the bar. The door was open and stepping inside Kate saw a small rectangular space, a desk, chair, large safe and a stack of IT equipment.

'He viewed everything in here' said Jenny. 'Liked his video games as well, strange for someone like him, you know old and fat, pub landlord. Codes for the CCTV were written on "stamp its" stuck to the wall. Harry had clearly found this a useful filing system because dozens of them filled every available wall space above and to the side of his desk.

'DC Lewis you and Jenny pop back to the bar and let's see what the viewing angle is on these cameras.' They returned to the part of the bar containing the second till. Jenny placed herself behind it while Damian resumed his seat in the alcove. It was perfect. Now for the footage.

Having enacted the requested piece of theatre, Damian rejoined Kate, whilst Jenny went about her chores, and there it was, just like Eve had said. Kate leapt from her seat grazing her knees on the desktop. Damian stood grinning like a fool, Jenny came running in. 'Did you get what you wanted?'

'You better believe it girl.' Damian in the mood for a hug took advantage of the situation and grabbed Jenny. Kate looked on disapprovingly, smiling deep inside.

'Right Lewis put the girl down, we need to get this written up and sent upstairs. Thank you so much for your help Jenny, it's going to help to make Eve a free woman, although there will be a few more questions we will need to answer before we get her back. She will be so relieved, ecstatic, when she finds out.

'Tell her we're thinking of her and I'll put a pint on the bar every night till she comes home.'

24. Recircling Crows

Andrei Micalovic had escaped. There was now an unexpected hole in his income. His early retirement would have to be put on hold. This upset him. However not all of his eggs were in one basket. He still had his small but profitable people trafficking business. Perhaps it was time to increase that particular side to his operations.

It was a shame about Adi. He had done everything he could for him. His was a stupid death. They had escaped the raid, leaving with seconds to spare. They would have been free. Sat in the tall grass thirty metres from the unit they had watched despairingly as armed officers surrounded the building.

They had listened to the shots, the shouts, the screams of terror. One of their men burst through a window sending shards of glass flying in all directions. Shadowy figures swept out through several exits. He ran, they followed.

Warnings were given to stop. He kept running. Shots were fired, passing so awfully close to the runaway, but deliberately missing. Fatefully another target was found. The foliage surrounding Andrei and his friend was riddled with metal, as bullets meant to prevent an unnecessary death caused one.

Andrei had been lucky. Adi had not. He had carried his friend for several miles, but he had lost too much blood. He had been a good friend a loyal business partner but there could be no loose ends. Andrei had to be certain. It had been quick.

The girls would say many things, but their "truths" would be difficult to prove. Their statements would be contradictory, confused, lacking a framework. Their drugged minds would ensure that. Their ignorance of even the time of day, let alone the actual day, he was sure would frustrate even the most dedicated of interrogators.

Andrei was shaken from his thoughts by the booming voice of an impassioned speaker. He had watched the man's performance but had little time for his words. Andrei had decided a long time ago that actions spoke so much louder.

'That's the problem with this town.' A rotund man in his fifties eyed the room. 'There are no morals anymore. Let nobody deny we are all guilty of what is happening on our doorsteps. We must stand up against the right wing extremists who in their hatred and Islamophobia, attack our culture and our religion.'

Councillor Saad Hassan let his words sink in. His audience were in his hands and he was enjoying every minute. He loved the power, the control, and his followers would ensure he retained it for a long time to come.

The speech or was it a lecture was coming to a close and Andrei edged closer as the room emptied.

'What are you doing here?'

'That's no way to treat a friend.' Andrei's eyes had narrowed, often the last thing some people noticed.

'Come with me.' Saad Hassan directed Andrei to a plain wooden door. 'You shouldn't be here.' They sat down on chairs in a small room with cracked walls and dust encrusted windows, a fading lamp bulb providing little light. In the centre of the round wooden table that separated them lay an ash tray full with cigarette ends, of various lengths.

'I heard about the demise of our business Andrei. There has

been no news of you or Adi. What happened?'

Andrei explained the events which had brought him to Hassan including the unfortunate shooting of Petrovic. Naturally, he missed out the finer details of his death.

'And now what?'

'We start again, but first we need to bring some more girls in, the rest you can leave to me.'

Saad Hassan blanched. He rubbed two of his fingers against his thumb and cricked his chubby neck. He cupped his chin in his right hand.

'We have to be smart, we need to let some time pass, make sure they are not aware of your luck. Then when the time is right come back to me and we will make some appropriate arrangements.'

Andrei bridled at the suggestion of a delay, but he knew Hassan was right. 'A couple of weeks then no more. In the meantime, I need some money. I will find a place to start again, get things ready for when you decide to lift your ass.'

'This is no way to talk to a friend, especially one whose help you need.' Hassan held a note of menace in his voice that did not go unnoticed by Andrei. There was also a smile on the man's face. 'How much do you need my friend?'

25. The Power Of Guilt

It wasn't the first time they had discussed it, but it had to be the last time, a decision was necessary.

'I can't let Eve Kendall go to prison for this. She tried to help me Yaz. My silence is ruining her life while we sit here wondering what to do. I'm going to confess.'

'She's just a copper Terry you have to think of us, of Tracy, she can't live without her dad.'

'Well she certainly can't live without her mum so it's a no brainer.'

They both sat down on a couch. They held hands like lovers, and like mourners united in grief. They both remembered the awful day that had led them to this moment, the emotions, smells, sounds.

It had been a lovely sunny day, unusual for the time of year. Tracy often played in the back garden, the walls too high for a small girl to climb, the gate lock out of reach. Locals used the back lane now and again and when someone passed by Tracy always had a barrage of words to amuse them with.

Today had been no different and the man had passed by before. He stopped and placed his hands on the arched top of the pale blue wooden gate. He spoke to the small girl whilst slyly examining the latch.

'How are you today young lady?'

Tracy was busy, her mind on her story, an adventure involving a friendly lion called "Billie" and an exceedingly small man that sat on the palm of her hand and said a lot of funny things. She reluctantly lifted her head. 'I'm fine, thank you.'

'What are you doing?'

'Playing.'

'Can I play with you?'

'Not really' the little girl thought to herself. She heard a click and looked up. The man had opened the gate, was in the garden, she was annoyed, she was playing, and he was interrupting.

'You're not supposed to be in my garden.' Tracy had been told so many times not to talk to strangers, but this man wasn't exactly a stranger she had seen him before. No one was allowed in the garden, but he was there. Perhaps everything was alright.

'What is your name?'

'Tracy.'

'Do you have adventures in your garden shed Tracy?'

'Sometimes but only with daddy.'

The man was closer. He smelt sweet, he smelt of her bath time soap, he offered her a small bag of chocolate buttons.

'You've got dirty nails.'

'Yes I have.' He was taken aback but turned the situation to his advantage. 'It's because I have been playing in my shed. It was fun.' The man watched her intently through small hazel eyes, one discoloured, bloodshot, spreading from the corner.

'What were you playing.' A small girls interest had been stirred.

'Would you like me to show you.' His arm was around the Tracy's shoulder, directing her to the shed, painted blue to match the garden gate.

'I'm not allowed in the shed without daddy.'

'You are today.' The shed was new and well ordered, no empty paint pots, random bits of wood, no musty aroma imprisoned within. Tracy waited expectantly to see what the man would do. There was silence, she did not like the look on his face. It had changed, he was different, sweating, no longer the smell of soap.

Tracy was frightened. She screamed.

Yaz was in the kitchen when she heard her daughter's cries of anguish. She peered through the window and saw no sign of her daughter. She raced through the door tripping over the step her apron flapping around her already trembling knees.

Another scream. A large figure silhouetted, framed in the window of the garden shed. No sign of Tracy. A crash, stumbling, heavy objects thudding to the ground. The door flew open a sobbing, fleeing girl rushing to escape, her arms held high in fear.

Yaz bounded toward her, smothering her tightly to her body . Nobody followed, the sobbing eased, the silence that followed was as frightening as the noise had been. Yaz examined her daughter's face, tear stained, streaks of dirt, nothing more. She was afraid to ask. She didn't want to leave her daughter, but she had to know what had happened to the man in the window.

'Sit here on the swing darling. Don't worry Mummy won't be long I just need to close the shed door, the nasty man has gone.'

Yaz walked hesitatingly toward the shed stopping to pick up a sharp rock from the side of the path. She stopped again. Should she ring for help? Be brave.

Terry arrived home late. Walking through the door he was met by his wife rushing toward him enveloping him in a tight embrace, her face a mess of tears and mascara. He held her for a minute before pushing her to arm's length. He looked into her eyes and held her again. Another minute passed. He tried again, his own eyes welling and hazy.

'What on earth's wrong Yaz.' She couldn't speak. She grabbed his hand and pulled him to the kitchen, out into the garden. She opened the door to the garden shed and shrank back slumping painfully to the floor where she stayed, tears once more cascading down her cheeks.

'Oh shit.' Terry sat down beside his wife, his arm wrapped around her shoulders in a futile attempt to bring some comfort. He let time slip by, fighting to create an explanation, waiting to be provided with one. 'In your own time Love.'

Eventually, still shocked, half composed Yaz looked for the words to describe the horror of her day. 'I heard screams. I saw a man in the shed. I ran, there was a lot of noise and Tracy came out. The man didn't. He must have fallen, his head, the nail.'

'It's the pervert from the swimming pool isn't it?'

'Yes.'

'Okay then we had better call the police. Clearly it was an accident and we haven't touched the body. You haven't touched it have you Yaz?'

The look on the face of his wife confirmed a twist to the story. 'Take a closer look Terry.'

Terry Frost closed his eyes and raised his head to the sky. He was scared, his wife's words had been cold. He peered once more around the shed door. He could see the back of the prone figure. A pool of dried blood could be seen in front of the body. A large nail stuck out a couple of inches from the leg of one of the benches, a jelly like substance suspended in air dangling from the spike.

He moved toward the body, bent over, and looked. A strange sight met his eye. The handle of one of his chisels protruded from the man's chest, the blade digging deep into flesh and bone. Terry groaned. 'Tell me again Yaz, all of it.'

'I'm so sorry Terry, I was terrified and so angry, such strength, such....' Yaz broke down once more.

'Take your time sweetheart. What's done is done I'll sort it, but I need to know Yaz.'

'I went in, there was blood on his face, he was moaning, moving slightly, and then he grabbed at me, I saw your chisel, grabbed it. It happened so quick.'

Neither of them had known what to do. Yaz had panicked. Now it was Terry's turn.

'Go indoors love, put the kettle on, make it hot and sweet. I'll be maybe an hour.'

'What are you going to do Terry? Don't do anything stupid for God's sake.'

'It's already been done Yaz. Off you go.'

He walked back through the house smiling briefly at his wife who had taken his advice and sat sipping her tea, numb with an experience she should not have had to endure. Terry drove his van down the back lane and returned to the shed. He opened a cupboard high on the wall. Every sinew of his body, every nerve in his brain told him what he was going to do was wrong, but his family came first. He retrieved a bag of plastic gloves from the lower shelf and put a pair on. He took a large knife from the top shelf, carefully handling the sheaf around the blade, using the cross guard to remove it. There were prints on the handle he didn't want to disturb. Terry Frost removed the chisel with difficulty, the flesh and muscles sucking it back in. Into its place he slid the knife applying pressure to the cross section. He had dragged the body to his van, hard work made easy by the adrenalin surging through his veins. He felt sick.

An hour later Terry Frost returned through the back door. Yaz looked up expectantly. Her husband strode past. 'Need a bath.' He came back downstairs thirty minutes later in his dressing gown, his hair wet, his face glowing from the warmth of the water he had immersed himself in. He opened the fridge door and grabbed a beer. Yaz snuggled up to him on the sofa. 'I'll clean up tomorrow love.'

26. When The Air Tastes Sweet

Eve had been waiting for some time. She had always thought the room she sat in, was a bit small, and good do with a spot of paint. Today it looked so much nicer. She was beginning to feel she had been there for an eternity, her experience had taught her patience, that was for sure.

At last the door opened and in walked DI Taylor. She stopped, her eyes getting larger by the second, astonishment slamming its way over her face. Her mouth went slack as she looked at Eve.

'What are you doing in my office?'

'He confessed.'

'Confessed? What do you mean confessed? Who confessed?

'God, this is worse than the interrogation room. Terry bloody Frost that's who.'

Kate couldn't help herself. She bent over and clamped Eve in a bear like hug gluing her to the chair. 'Damian in here now.'

'Wow that was quick. I knew you were good Ma'am, but I haven't even written the blooming report.' Damian's surprise was as big as Kate's had been, but his smile was even bigger. Laughter and tears of various levels littered the room for a few precious moments before understanding dawned.

Eve wiped a small droplet from her mouth. 'What report?'

Damian and Kate looked at each other and raised the volume

of laughter several notches.

Eve realised she hadn't learned to be quite as patient as she had thought and waited, mouth slightly agape, foot and fingers tapping, tongue rooted to the top of her mouth. Eventually Kate straightened up, took a deep breath, and broke their news.

'We, well actually DC Lewis here, proved you had a meeting with Frost. We have CCTV evidence of him giving you the knife and then pocketing it.' Kate explained how Lewis had used his experience of working in dodgy pubs during his student days to find a second camera nobody knew about.

'Well I'm buggered.' Said Eve. I wouldn't put it past the old sod having one in the loos as well. Thank you so bloody much Harry, get well soon. And thank you both, I always believed in you Kate, and you, young man, have really come up trumps for me. I owe you big style. Both of you and I won't forget.'

The smiles in the room were a mixture of relief, pride and friendship but they could only last for so long before things would become embarrassing. The knock on the door came at exactly the right time. Kate looked up to see whom had interrupted

'Talk to me Tess.'

I've spoken to the SFOs who carried out the raid at the industrial site. As far as they are concerned nobody was able to escape the building. They are either in cells or dead. However, the girls insist that the main men who they knew as Andrei Micalovic and Adi Petrovic are neither dead nor in custody.'

'Which can only mean they weren't there when we arrived.'

'Seems like the only answer Ma'am'

'So where the bloody hell are they.'

'Well Ma'am several of the girls have told me they were brought to the building in Loxborough via the coast. Usual story tricked into believing they were coming to work legally in the UK in bars and hotels and by the time they understand what's going on they have had their passports taken away and have been scared shitless. Apparently, this Adi was the worst, raping anyone he wanted, anytime he chose, and he wasn't gentle.

'And your point is DC Campbell.'

'Perhaps they controlled the trafficking as well or at least played a part in it. Maybe they will look to start up again.'

'Interesting. Good work Tess. Stay on it. I'll request some help from the drugs squad. You might need them to interview the men.'

'Brilliant Ma'am and there's one more thing.' Tess paused. Kate sighed. If only pausing for effect was deleted from the manual things would be done a damn sight quicker.

'A couple of the girls are British Ma'am, Yorkshire born and bred. They stick out like sore thumbs from the rest of the girls.'

'And how did they get themselves into this mess.'

DC Campbell grinned from ear to ear. 'Via grooming gangs Ma'am.'

'Now that's what I call a breakthrough. Listen keep talking to them. DC Lewis can join you. I've seen him in action with the ladies. If anyone can get through to them, he will. Great work Tess.

27. Hindrance Or Help?

The woman spoke first. 'We've read the papers, we've watched your television interviews. You care.'

'In short we think we can trust you.' Her male companion added his tuppence worth, a look of sincerity glowing on his face. Kate chewed her lip. She had an aversion to sincerity. More often than not it proved worthless. She had met people like this before. They oozed righteousness, demanded tolerance, and suggested humility. Underneath they were fickle, chose when and where to apply their high morals, happily discarding them if they didn't temporarily fit their agenda.

'And you are?' queried Kate.

'Alison Coombes.' Again, the woman spoke first.

'And I'm Leroy Obei.' To Kate they sounded like they were introducing a game show or completing a news bulletin.

Kate directed them to a couple of chairs. 'Take a seat.' She moved behind her desk and sat down facing her visitors. 'How can I help?'

'Well actually we're here to help you.' The man spoke with a very cultured English accent. He was tall, slim, handsome. Large brown eyes dominated his perfectly formed oval face. He had removed his oatmeal overcoat but not his cream scarf. Cream pullover as well noticed Kate.

'And then perhaps you could help us.' The woman's voice was slightly irritating or perhaps it was just her words. She was short, so was her hair, she had a bland face matched by her clothes. Kate hadn't taken to her.

Kate raised her eyebrows, chewed on her lip once more and waited.

The two visitors were clearly uncomfortable with the silence that followed Alison Coombe's words. They had expected a reply. The strain told and Alison continued.

'For some time now, we have been receiving reports of girls as young as ten being abused by gangs of foreigners. We have been able to bring together people from all ages, cultures and even religions who are determined to end this vile practice. It is an exceedingly small minority who perform this evil and we want to offer you our help to bring the perpetrators to justice.'

Kate coughed. While she and her team had been effectively blundering around with no end result it appeared an underworld of "do gooders" was forming a resistance. 'That' thought Kate 'is all I need.'

'Our community network has taken some time to build.' Leroy took the lead. 'After a great deal of hard work and no small amount of pain both personal and professional....'

Kate was losing interest and began hoping this, no doubt well meaning, young man, would get to the point, so she could get on with catching criminals. She was mentally pleading with him to leave out the "self" bits and move on. Why did charity workers and the ilk need to stress their great works on behalf of mankind? For goodness sake the clue was in the title "Charity". Kate realised she was rambling to herself and regained focus.

'.....and as a result we now have over one hundred and sixty volunteers feeding us information.'

'Impressive.' Unfortunately, Kate in giving way to her musings had missed the thrust of the speech. She began to dig. 'One hundred and sixty volunteers. How confident are you in this information?' She had used all of her experience to open the conversation back up without admitting she hadn't been listening.

Alison Coombes took over. 'Our volunteers have for the last three months been helping us to plot the movements of groups of young people throughout the area. We can now tell you where they go, when they go, what time they go and the routes they take.'

Kate was impressed. It was rather, hiding behind the curtains stuff, but it could be useful.

'Of course, a lot of the information is innocent enough, shopping, going to school, straightforward meeting up for good healthy fun.' Leroy was back. 'Once you eliminate that you get some remarkably interesting data, and it leads to just a couple of places.'

They both sat back in their chairs on the conclusion of Leroy's sentence looking like the cats that got the cream, but only for a few fleeting moments before Alison resumed. 'And we are going to do something about it.'

Kate could only surmise what that "something" might be. Coffee mornings, car boot sales, mini marathons or any of the other fund raising events such groups as Alison and Leroy's organised to bring in funds, money to enable their two bit "Stairway to Heaven" to continue.

'What is wrong with you today' Kate asked herself. 'Get a grip, try being professional, show some respect, for goodness sake.'

'Okay. Thank you both. Can I just ask some questions? These routes where do they lead?'

'Parklands.' The word was offered in unison. 'A café and a house' said Alison providing more detail.

'At what time of day are these routes taken?'

'There is no rhyme or reason to the movement with regard to times. But here's the thing, groups of mainly girls pass through the surrounding area to reach their destination but few if any return the same way, and when they do, it's just the odd one or two, not large groups.'

This was certainly intriguing, and Kate began to appreciate their efforts a little bit more.   'And what are you going to do about it?'

'We are going to organise a meeting with some particularly important people.'

Kate lost interest again. She would thank them for the information and allow her team to spend a day researching it. 'Well thank you, again. Please let me know how your meeting went.' Kate rose extending her hand, already thinking of the things she needed to be doing.

'Wait you don't understand.' It was Leroy again. 'You're coming to the meeting. This is big, powerful, you must help us.'

'I'm sorry. You have obviously been working extremely hard and I truly appreciate your information. I can assure you my team will follow it up. But I need witnesses, pure and simple. Facts not hearsay. I need times, places, names. Can you provide any of this?'

Alison Coombes looked at her associate. They spoke with their eyes. Leroy Obei leaned forward. Three or four over emphasised movements and sighs later he came to the point. 'We can do better than that. We will introduce you to Ali Khalid.

Kate sucked her lip. She had always wondered why people did this when they found themselves in front of a police officer with what they assumed was important information. It was like watching EastEnders. Drama with no substance. Ali bloody Khalid, well that's all right then. Her initial burst of frustration over, Kate hoped there was more substance.

'And who is this Ali Khalid?'

'He is the leader of the mosque in Parklands.'

Now that, thought Kate is much more like it.

28. When Worlds Collide

'I get it. We're all pissed off.' Kate had faced a wall of negativity from her team. She had been given time to smash her way through it, they had not, and she now had a job to do to lift her people, ignite the spark and catch the bad guys.

'How many times have I told you to learn from your mistakes. How many times do we have doors closed in our face only to get back up and open ten more, and how do we find those doors to open? We get out and ask questions. We look for signs. We pile up the evidence and most important of all we follow our instincts.

'And as it happens, the Lord has provided, sort of.'

DI Kamani you will accompany me. We have a meeting with a Mullah. DC Campbell, DC Lewis you are going to continue to make friends with the girls we rescued

'Any questions?'

Two men entered the mosque. They could not have been more different. One was tall, thin, boarding on ill, hook nosed, grey strands of hair, larger than normal ears. The other was of a darker complexion, of medium height, a full head of black hair and eyes that might be considered mysterious.

'Good morning. Thank you for coming. My name is Ali Khalid I am the Imam for this mosque and this, is Reverend Edward King.'

Kate nodded in acknowledgement. 'DI Taylor and DS Kamani,

pleased to meet you.'

Edward and I have joined together to confront the evil that stalks our streets and threatens the daughters of our communities. I refer of course to the "grooming gangs" about which we hear so much but which we can never bring to justice. Why can we not do this DI Taylor?'

Kate thought for a moment before answering. 'A lack of will I'm afraid but certainly not from my team who are desperate to prosecute these criminals. Unfortunately, it seems, and I hope you don't mind me being blunt Imam, the leaders of the Muslim community in general are not prepared to denounce the men behind it.'

'I appreciate you being candid, and I accept your point DI Taylor, but to many the actions of these vile men is allowed by their religious beliefs.'

Kate had heard this argument before. 'And are they?' She needed to know how far this man's stated conviction to stop the gangs went.

'The subject of rape is complicated in Islamic law DI Taylor, as there is not a law specifically against it. It comes under the laws which forbid sex outside of marriage, "Zina". Islam considers rape a sin and the punishment can be death by stoning. The problem is if the case cannot be proved it is likely the woman is the one who will be stoned for having sex outside of marriage.

To get a conviction in a Muslim country there have to be four male witnesses, or, the rapist has to confess. Furthermore, if less than four witnesses appear those who have made the accusations will be accused of slander and punished themselves. Not much chance of a conviction I am afraid. The Imam paused and thought before restarting his brief explanation of the intricacies of Muslim law.

'And then you have the rape of an infidel and it is here that the, in my opinion false excuses some followers use, are born. Be assured the vast majority of enlightened followers of Islam do not condone rape or any form of abuse of women. There are however sections of society that consider it their right. Unfortunately, they contend that if they see an infidel who is in their opinion, shall we say, underdressed, then she should be punished.

The Qur'an allows for the rape of slaves or captive women. As these are likely to be infidels the inference can be made that Allah allows the rape of foreign women. This inference I can assure you is not made by any right thinking Muslim and my intention is to prove it.'

'I've heard much of this before. It could be seen as a very convenient excuse to look the other way could it not?' Kate hated the proffered explanation uttered by Khalid and could not help baiting him.

'It is time for our religions to join together and try to bring an end to the division these so called grooming gangs are causing between our peoples.' Reverend King intervened to prevent an escalation. He had taken centre stage and was happy to show off his preaching skills. Kate listened politely. In two weeks' time, my congregation and the worshippers of the mosque will, on completion of their services, converge on the Town Hall and not only show our solidarity against the abuse of young girls in this area, but also the way in which a blind eye is being cast by the authorities.'

'If there is so much anger about this problem why just your church Reverend and your mosque Imam?' Rashi's question was a good one.

'Little acorns, young man, little acorns.' The Reverend Edward King smiled patronisingly cherishing the clever words he had chosen.

Kate was intent on having the last word on the subject. She thanked the two men of God and wished them well in their efforts stressing her appreciation for their proposed fight against the abuse inherent in the community. She and Rashi moved toward the doors. Before leaving Kate turned.

'I'm afraid little acorns take rather a long time to grow Reverend King. I'm afraid the girls on the street don't usually live long enough to see the end result.'

He watched her go and determined to pray harder.

29. The Awakening

It's one of those things you can't explain. The local pub is, to so many people a hub, a family, a place to remember and to forget. There was always a smell to it that comforted, a certain light and a welcoming aura. What was it that made such places special? Eve had decided long ago it was the fact a pub was a constant, it didn't change, the one part of you that you could rely on to stand firm amidst a sea of eternal chaos. A sanctuary.

It was quiet tonight. It would give her time to think. Tuesdays were always primetime for a good old natter with Jenny. Tonight, would be different, a time for reflection. But first there had to be a pinch of banter, it was only right, a necessity.

'Lucky you have such good friends Eve.' Jenny had settled down from the hugging and back slapping, even the moisture in her eyes had left. 'They were determined to help you, they would never have let you go down. They totally believed in you girl. And that copper Lewis, he can frisk me any time.'

'Damian?'

'Yes, the big black bloke. Gorgeous.' Jenny made her final word stretch as she thought back to the clever guy who had cracked the case.

'I don't think he's really your type Jenny. He's really nice.'

'I can change. Anyway, it's about time I settled down. Time to find a decent one and if it doesn't work out at least I would have got my hands on those biceps.'

Eve chuckled. 'You're incorrigible.'

'I'll take your word for that.' Jenny poured another glass of lager. 'Lime with this one?'

'No thanks.'

'Thank goodness for that I thought you'd gone funny on me.'

Eve laughed again. 'Thank the lord for people like Jenny' she thought to herself smiling at her friend in total appreciation for who she was. Jenny was a "real" person. She would let you down every now and again, who didn't, but when you needed her, she would be there, every time. She also knew her customers, some said better than they knew themselves. She sensed Eve needed some "My" time. She moved away without being obvious, leaving Eve alone with her thoughts.

Eve had been brooding ever since they had told her Frost had confessed. It didn't sit right with her. She had relived every minute, or at least every minute that mattered, in the sequence of events that had taken her to desolation and back, and the nagging doubt persisted.

'He didn't do it.'

Jenny looked at her friend. She had been slightly concerned about her ever since her awful experience had come to an end. She just wasn't the same. Not surprising being accused of a murder you didn't commit, especially when all the evidence said you had done it. Thank God for friends thought Jenny.

'Sorry Eve, you what?'

'Terry Frost did not kill that man.'

Jenny expected more. It didn't come. She decided to wait for Eve to explain, instead Eve sipped her beer and peered into the far reaches of the pub. Jenny didn't push it further. She picked up a glass and began to wipe it rather a lot more than she needed to. The suspense was too much.

'Okay I give up why didn't he do it?'

Eve stared at Jenny vacantly. She wasn't ready to expand on her statement, there were things that she still had to think through, but her mind was virtually made up. More minutes passed in silence. Jenny had consigned herself to the background where she would wait for Eve to spark back to reality. It seemed like an age but finally Eve was ready to elaborate.

'Why would Terry Frost go to such an effort to frame me and then confess? He totally set me up. That took time and planning. He would have almost certainly succeeded except for Kate and Damian finding the second camera. If he had confessed after they had reported their findings that would have been one thing, but he didn't, he confessed before he knew what they had found. Why Jenny?'

'Guilt?' Jenny had no idea what the answer was. She was hoping Eve did. Jenny wanted to talk about her latest shopping trip. Eve didn't.

Eve considered Jenny's reply. Guilt was not what Frost had shown when he attacked the guy at the swimming pool. Under different circumstances he might have killed him. Or perhaps not. Was Frost all mouth and no trousers?

'No Jenny not guilt.'

As Eve left the bar she was halted by a final call from Jenny. 'I would really like to thank your police friend for helping you. Could you arrange that.'

Eve stopped. 'Only if you promise to be gentle.'

Jenny laughed 'No chance of that.'

30. The Visitor

'Bloody hell what are you doing here. You're the last person I would expect a visit from.'

Eve waited for the door to close behind her.

'Listen Eve, believe it or not I'm sorry for everything I've put you through. I don't expect you to forgive me, but I am truly sorry.'

Eve listened. This confirmed her beliefs. Why was he apologising. This guy was a pussy.

'You didn't do it Terry and I'm going to prove it.'

Terry Frost's mouth went slack, his eyes opened wide, he struggled for a response. 'Of course I did. I've told you I'm sorry, now just leave me alone.' He slumped down on to the single mattress the one real comfort any prison cell possessed.

'You didn't do it Terry.' Eve repeated herself but with more emphasis.

'Look drop it for fuck's sake drop it.'

Eve looked at the man in front of her. Everything about him was wrong, his responses, his posture, his protestations. The guy was innocent. He was protecting someone, someone close and that narrowed the field right down.

'Help me Terry. I'm going to find out anyway. Work with me.'

'Look the bastard deserved to die, he molested my kid, that comes with a price and he paid.' It was a strongly delivered statement, but it was driven by despair, not conviction. It didn't add up.

DI Kendall tried to make eye contact. She failed. Frost's eyes held the sheen of tears. This was all wrong. There would be no further point in Eve remaining. The breakthrough was close, she could feel it, but not today.

Her next visit came soon. 'This is the last time I am going to allow a visit from you Eve.'

DI Kendall recognised a call for help when she heard one.

'Don't worry, it will be Terry.'

Terry Frost shifted in surprise and an unexpected feeling of disappointment. 'Oh good.' His words failed to carry any degree of conviction.

'Listen Terry I know what happened.'

'No, you don't, I mean, what are you on about?'

He was right of course she was guessing, she was here on a "fishing" expedition, but she was certain she was close. She decided on shock tactics. 'Your wife killed him didn't he.' It was a statement not a question, designed to cause alarm. It worked.

He hesitated, regained control, and answered. 'Don't be bloody stupid.'

'Maybe I can help.' Eve probed, offering hope might work.

'Look just shut up, leave me alone.' Her leaving wasn't what he wanted, he needed to talk to someone, needed to explain. He had an ache for closure.

'Why did you set me up in the pub Terry? Eve titled her head enquiringly.

'I didn't love. I honestly didn't. You helped me, I picked up the knife and left. I had no intention to kill anybody let alone frame you. Things changed.'

'I understand that Terry. Family comes first. If you can't believe in them you have nothing left to believe in. Right?' Terry Frost noted the tinge of sadness in her voice, the first sign of any sort of weakness he had ever seen in this hard headed woman. The people who knew her reckoned she had bigger balls than most men. She certainly behaved like it most of the time.

'Listen Terry I am not holding any grudge. I learned long ago keeping things tucked up inside only destroys what little empathy we have for others. I am trying to help. I know you didn't do it. Bloody hell Terry work with me.' Her voice had become hard. Desperation drove the change.

Deep down inside he wanted to talk to somebody, he needed to confide in someone he could trust. If he was going to take the blame, he desperately needed for there to be somebody who knew the truth, who knew there was a good side to him. He wasn't a killer, but he would play the part, for those he loved. If someone else shared the secret he was sure he would feel better.

'Terry, tell them the truth. Call it self-defence. Yaz could go free you won't.'

'I thought you were the copper round here Eve but you certainly ain't acting like one. Think of it. Theoretically like. Say Yaz did kill him, in self defence like you say. You're forgetting we moved the body, framed you. You're missing out the fact that....' He stopped short of saying too much.

'Go on Terry.'

Frost looked long and hard at Eve fingering his right ear between finger and thumb. He licked his dry lips he didn't like where this was going and yet he already felt better for his veiled confession of events. 'Eve tell me I can trust you. Tell me this goes no further.'

'My word Terry. If at the end of this, you ask me to keep my mouth shut, it will stay shut. I promise, I will walk away from it.'

'Point is this. You're right. I have admitted killing him to protect my wife and daughter. What do you think will happen to me?

Truthfully.'

'With a good beak anywhere between six and ten years, halved for good behaviour.'

'And if Yaz pleads self-defence.'

'Might get off, might do a couple of years.'

'And me Eve, what would I get for trying to cover things up, perverting the course of justice. Blaming it on you. What would I get Eve?'

The penny dropped. Terry Frost was not prepared to take the gamble that they might both end up behind bars, their child left in care.

Eve stood up walked over to Terry Frost and hugged him, tears in her eyes. 'I wish you had been my dad Terry.' She held him at arm's length a look of respect in her wet eyes.

'As agreed, this is my last visit. Goodbye mate, good luck. If you change your mind let me know.'

Frost watched as she headed for the door his face a mess of emotion.

Eve turned. 'Tell Yaz if she needs anything, I'm there.' The door opened. She left.

31. Chance Meeting.

Damian could not imagine why Eve Kendall was so attached to her local pub. It felt completely different in the night time to how he remembered it on his first visit which seemed a long time ago now.

'Hello officer.' Jenny threw a flirtatious smile in his direction. 'What's a nice boy like you doing in a place like this.'

'I'm off duty so please call me Damian and less of the nice please, I have an image to maintain you know. Eve asked me to meet her for a drink as a sort of thank you I guess.'

'Yes, I know she just rang. Asked me to apologise like mad and pour you a drink. She can't make it.' Jenny of course knew very well Eve had never intended to be there, she was just doing a favour for a friend. 'What would you like it's on Eve.'

Damian was in two minds. He was disappointed and pissed off at the same time. Still one drink and stop off at the Union on the way home.

'Lager shandy please.'

'Are you driving?'

'No taxi.'

'Then you are having a proper drink the more expensive the better, that will teach our Eve to leave you high and dry with little old me.' Jenny was going to work this one for all it was worth.

'Alright you can leave out the lemonade.'

'There was one other thing Eve said.' This was the line Jenny had been looking forward to. 'Eve's in the darts team, that leaves us short.' She offered Damian an amusing smile, her eyes sparkling with expectation. Now Damian understood. Various ways to gain revenge on his so called friend raced through his brain. He looked again at Jenny and decided things weren't quite so bad after all.

'Yes, I can play darts. I can play darts very, very well thank you.'

32. Moving On

The team had been assembled for a review of their progress which was in Kate's eyes a rather optimistic title considering the reality of the situation on all fronts. She gave herself a swift slap on the face, negativity had no place in the room today.

'What was that for Ma'am.' Damian sat with a confused look on his face. Kate for a mere second had forgotten where she was.

'I had forgotten something. I do that to remind myself. As I very rarely forget things you will not have seen me do it before.' Kate was pleased with how quickly she had come up with that one.

'Let's start with you DS Kamani. How did the army of the righteous fare?'

'Bit of a waste of time I'm afraid Ma'am. They marched on the Town Hall, well at least around thirty Christians and perhaps a hundred Muslims, but it wasn't exactly what you would call a success, more a complete lack of interest. Seems grooming gangs are not a subject for this fine upstanding town of ours. It's almost like they believe if they ignore it, it doesn't exist. A bit like blooming pedestrians who think if they look the other way you won't run them over.'

'Yes, so damned annoying. It's so tempting to put your foot on the accelerator and give them a scare.' Damian had taken up the theme with a vigour that surprised even him. 'Not that I would of course.'

Kate stared pleadingly at the floor, perhaps it would be so good as to swallow her up. 'DC Campbell tell me something I want to hear.'

'Will do Ma'am. Would you like me to tell the boys about my success with leads on the grooming gangs, or the prostitution racket Ma'am.'

If Kate had the strength she would have given Tess a strongly worded put down. She didn't. She decided to let DC Campbell have her head, very briefly. She probably deserved it.

'Okay let's stay with the grooming gangs.' Tess explained to her colleagues how by using her amazing skills she had become firm friends with several of the girls now staying in a hostel who had been rescued from prostitution. 'I can't take all the credit, only most of it, because DC Lewis did play a small part, mainly as eye candy for the girls.' Even Damian laughed at that one.

Kate thought how Tess Campbell had come on in leaps and bounds especially since owning up to her previous underhand position as a mole. It seemed to have taken a big weight from her shoulders. She was pleased with the transformation.

Finally, Tess came to the point of her report. 'Two of the girls arrived at the "whorehouse", Kate cringed at the use of the phrase, 'via a grooming gang. It was almost as if the gang sold them to the eastern Europeans. They have also described an Asian guy who seems to have links with both operations. They know who he is, say he is a very important figure in the town but are still too scared to give us the name.'

'I'll get it, nobody can resist the charms of DC Lewis for long.'

'Or his annoying little traits'. Kate brought Damian back to earth but hadn't burst his bubble.

'No honestly Ma'am they love me I will get it.'

Tess stepped in quickly to save Damian from a DI Taylor broadside. 'Any questions?'

That was Kate's line. 'Bloody hell you two, you're worse than the Chuckle Brothers. Still you've made me smile and saved your bacon. Carry on DC Campbell.'

Tess further explained that some of the other girls were certain the two leaders of the sex gang had escaped on the night of the raid and as they had a part in the trafficking that brought most of the girls to the industrial estate in the first place they were probably still in business.

'Well done Tess. Thank you. We seem to have an overlap in the two investigations. Tess you and Damian continue with the girls, let's get something tied down.' Kate stopped in mid-sentence. 'Don't even think about it DC Lewis. DS Kamani see if you can get any information about the trafficking that might be taking place around here. Talk to other units, check the archives, newspapers, anything and everything. Where's bloody DS Kendall when you need her.'

As she was finishing her tirade the door swung open. 'Do I hear my name being taken in vain?'

'Eve, DS Kendall are you back?' Kate hoped she was but worried this was only a fleeting visit and that Eve was not ready to return quite yet.

'Oh yes' said DS Kendall the old sparkle springing from her eyes. 'I'm back and I'm in need of a punch bag so point me at the bad guys.'

33. New Nesting Grounds

Compared to their last operation this was bordering on luxurious. 'You have done well my friend.'

'With the help of your generosity Saad.'

'That is true and if I say so myself the merchandise is of a better quality is it not?'

'It's true you have exceeded all expectations.'

'Then I suggest you look after it better this time, learn to be a better master, fewer bodies ending up in rivers, less profits thrown away.'

They grinned. Saad Hassan slapped Andrei Macalovic on the back a couple of times. 'Show me more.'

The two men embarked on a tour of the building. Another industrial site, a more modern building but still tucked away on the far perimeter. This time three roads allowed it to be approached more easily even though it was situated behind the main estate road. Their building comprised of three units. The basement walls had new doors installed, holes in walls having been knocked through. Any raid would be unaware of this and escape would be easier than it had been before. This was a long way from the Loxborough set up, clean rooms, new beds and bedding, and an entertainments lounge, a long pole centre stage to cater for the more exotic behaviour of some of the girls.

'Remember Andrei, these girls are different, they don't need drugging or beating, they are not slaves, they are willing. In six months, they will have paid their dues and they will be free, if that's what they want, and then if they leave, we will re-stock. It's practically legal.' Hassan considered his words amusing. Macalovic smiled politely.

Sitting around the "lounge" a dozen young women sat talking in several different languages. They were well dressed, none of them could be described as anything but attractive. Andrei nodded approvingly to himself, he would be back home sooner than he had hoped. A couple more weeks and they could open. In the meantime, he was in need of some good men, and some subtle publicity.

He needn't have worried. He found it quite incredible how word soon spread and yet still remained confined to those who would be interested. He worried how long the operation could thrive before somebody spoke to the wrong person or a quiet conversation was overheard. Saad Hassan had talked of continuing, of changing the girls every six months. Andrei would be gone as soon as enough money had been accumulated and shipped home, and then Hassan could pick up the pieces.

Girls soon began to trickle through the door to top up those that had been supplied by Hassan. They were the same tired looking, drug ruined waifs and strays that men like Andrei took full advantage of. He would see how they scrubbed up. They could offer their wares round the back of the building, a nice little extra income just for him, and a cheap alternative for the clients. The boys he turned away, they sickened him.

It was a building, but it wasn't home. A refuge, a stopping point until the next stage of a life that was not envied by anyone. Irena was here, for now, along with the other girls. They were slowly leaving, going back into the world they knew, the only world that would accept them. Irena had no intention to live that way anymore. She had seen a way out, a different way and she was going to take it.

DCs Lewis and Campbell had been frequent visitors. They were here again at her request, no doubt some tittle tattle picked up during hours of boredom would be relayed to them, unconfirmed reports, more an excuse for company than a helping hand.

Damian didn't mind he had become fond of her in a brotherly sort of way. Tess on the other hand was feeling frustrated, so much promised, so little gained.

'So why the excitement Irena. Do you have some news?' Damian accompanied his words with a warm smile. Irena felt something she hadn't had the joy of experiencing for so long, she knew the police officer cared, he didn't want her like other men, he just treated her with respect with tenderness and it was appreciated.

'Two of the girls left during the night. They were talking about a new place opening. Different they said than last time. Girls could come and go, no forced drugs, no violence and good money. I thought you would want to know.'

'Did they say where?' Tess was more direct than Damian would have liked. The girl needed coaxing, she needed to feel she was helping, part of something.

'Twenty minutes on the train. That's all.'

DC Lewis took over quickly not wanting Tess's lack of people skills to kill this off before it had started. The girl required time. 'Irena did they say when it was opening. Is it open now? Think carefully, take your time.'

'No they didn't but another girl, Katya is planning to visit the place later today. I could go with her if it would help you Damian.'

Tess could hardly contain her excitement. Damian made sure she did. Holding his hand up to stall her unfettered curiosity he moved to sit beside Irena. 'Yes Irena, it would help but I need to know you will be safe if you go with her. I will only be comfortable if I am able to follow you and if you promise to turn around anytime you feel unsafe.'

Irena was like putty in his hands, she demurred to him like a young girl in love, He was her knight in shining armour and she would sell her soul for him if only she still had one.

Damian could not understand why Tess was so reluctant to pair up with him for this trip. As far as he could see it was right up her street and yet she refused, saying DI Taylor had given her a load of office work to plough through. Never mind Rashi was a good replacement and it felt a bit more comfortable having a DS alongside, somebody to make the calls if and when they came.

It had been easy to follow the two girls on the train but the fact they chose to walk to the potential new "brothel" made for hard work both in the foot slog they were having to endure and the difficulty in avoiding being obvious, trailing as they were in the wake of the girls along what were becoming pretty much empty roads.

'These two are like blooming packhorses, they just keep going, must be hard as nails' moaned Damian.

'Too much of your mum's cooking and not enough time in the gym if you ask me Lewis. Look at that gut on you.' Damian was rather proud of his semi six pack and anyway it was his feet that were hurting not his stomach.

Finally, the girls stopped.

'Why have we stopped?' Irena stood still as her friend turned her head and shoulders taking in a full three hundred and sixty degree view of the landscape.

'We're supposed to be very careful. Apparently, they are quite nervous of being discovered, many of their clients are shall we say upstanding figures in the community.' They both giggled like schoolgirls. 'Down here I think.'

The two officers followed cautiously. Luckily one side of the road had not been built on, providing a good cover of long grass from which they could watch their guides. Even so they were still visible and would have to be careful.

Suddenly the girl leading Irena turned about. 'No this isn't it.' She stood still viewing her surroundings like a hunting dog sniffing for its prey.

Her actions totally wrong footed the policemen. In their haste to remain undiscovered they simultaneously lost their footing falling backwards down the slope they had been traversing. They fell in a heap, inches apart. It was their turn to be amused.

Katya grabbed Irena's arm. 'This way.' She moved swiftly down a side street, turned left down another narrow road, and dashed into an open door straight into the arms of an extremely large man in a very natty suit.

'What's the rush?' He looked down at them his pale grey eyes glinting in a manner too sinister for Irena's liking.

Katya spoke quickly. 'We were told to be careful, make sure we weren't being followed.'

'Were you being followed.'

'No but like I said, we were making sure.' Katya looked at him exuding confidence and harbouring total fear.

'Good.' The man's voice boomed at them. 'Up the stairs.' He pointed the way with his finger, or at least half a finger, the knuckle upwards missing. They obeyed immediately and the adventure had begun.

'Bollocks where did they go.' Damian had managed to get back up the slope first and the girls were nowhere to be seen. Rashi clambered up beside him spitting grass and rubbing mud from his scratched hands.

'No idea. We can't look for them it might put us all in danger. We go back up the road and wait. They must be here somewhere we weren't out of action that long.'

The room they found themselves in wasn't what they had expected. They were stunned, it was brilliant. They had expected some sort of improvement on the place they had been held in before. The outside hadn't raised their hopes to high, but this. They could work here no doubt about that. And that's where the smiles ended. Walking toward them was Andrei Micalovic and their fleeting joy had turned to anger, fear, and disgust.

'So you want to come and work here. Have you any experience?' The girls fear subsided slightly. He clearly didn't recognise either of them. Why should he, they had been trash, mere objects for other people's lust, to him they had been nothing. Of course, they also had changed from when he had last set eyes on them. They were no longer in a drug induced state, bruised and dirty.

'Depends' said Katya. 'What's on offer.'

Andrei shook his head. 'You have spirit. I like that.' His next action suggested he did not as he grabbed her by the throat and looked deep into her soul. 'You will work your way up until one day you may find yourself twirling around that pole. Until then you will do anything I ask.' The room had gone silent. Girls stood watching in disbelief. Andrei released her from his grip and as if nothing had happened spoke in a softer, kinder voice, a voice they had not heard him use before. 'Or, you can leave.'

'We will leave.' Katya spoke with defiance. Irena required information or else this had all been a waste of time. 'When do you open?'

'So, this little bird is still interested in singing, is she?' Andrei bent down to take a closer look at her. She seemed familiar.

'I might be.' Irena couldn't help the slight tremor in her voice. 'If the pay is right.'

'We open soon, a week from Friday. Come back then and I will find a place for you.'

'Come on Irena.' The girls tried hard not to run, their resilience had been tested and was about to collapse. They disappeared down the stairs and were thankful for the fresh air that engulfed their lungs as they half walked, half ran away from the newly created brothel.

'Irena.' Andrei Micalovic said the name out loud. 'That's where I know her from' his voice lowered. He would most definitely find a place for her. It would not be one she would like.

The two girls wondered where the police officers had gone. Irena in particular felt vulnerable without the large presence of Damian. They both began to feel goose bumps on their arms, small shivers down their spines. It could have gone better this afternoon, perhaps they were being followed, it certainly felt as if they were.

Kamani and Lewis shadowed them watching when permittable from parallel running roads. They would wait to reunite with the girls until far away from any potentially inquisitive eyes. When they did connect it was unexpected for all four of them. The girls fleetingly out of sight had taken a turning that took them straight into the paths of their guardian angels.

The shock they all experienced was quickly replaced by relief. Irena threw herself into the arms of DC Lewis. She held him close. She was safe.

'I can't go back.' Irena was looking up at Damian her eyes wet with fear her body trembling with something more. DC Lewis unravelled himself.

'You don't have to.'

'You can bloody well include me in that' announced Katya. The pig almost choked me to death. He is an animal.'

'Nobody needs to visit there again' confirmed DS Kamani. He hesitated, not wishing to seem unsympathetic. 'Did you learn anything about when it will open.' It was a hopeful question, a positive response not expected considering the state of the girls.

'In three days, Friday night. Now let's go.' Katya strode off leaving the others to follow in her wake. 'You can buy us a beer before we catch the train, it is deserved.'

It had been a successful day's police work. Funny at times to be sure, but deeply serious and disturbing in its revelations. He was tired but satisfied with their efforts and the results they had produced. He would be glad to settle down in front of the TV a nice bowl of lamb saag on his lap. A chapatti, that would be welcome as well.

Before he could touch the doorbell the door was opened, a face he knew and loved so much appeared in front of him, except it was a different face, same features, but no smile, no joy, only eyes made red with tears.

'Ma?' Rashi was shaken at the sight of his mother, alarm written on his face, fear in his eyes.

'Your father Rashi. He is dead.' The words had faltered but been delivered. Rashi froze, slumped to the floor, and hugged his mother's legs. He could not stay there long. He was now the head of the house an example had to be shown. He rose and guided his weeping mother back inside.

So many thoughts raced through his head, how, where, when. Why hadn't he been contacted. The restaurant, his family, the funeral, his dad, that wonderful, unique man.

A Muslim funeral left no time for Rashi to feel his grief, that would have to come later. Things needed to be done, and they had to be carried out correctly. His father's wonderful life would ensure his place in Paradise of that he was sure. He had been a man of integrity and loyalty. He had been honest and reliable, loving, and right thinking. In the meantime, there were many things to organise and observe, "Gushl", the washing of the body, and "Kafan" the shrouding. Rashi tried to remember the correct order of the washing, was it upper right first, yes, he was sure it was.

He stopped himself going further. He knew he was in a state of panic, he had to slow down, he had to be in control.

He would need time and that was short. Janazah had to take place within 24 hours. He would ask for more time since the death had been so sudden. He would need another forty days for the grieving. The restaurant, what would become of it, a choice would have to be made. He must let his boss know. He sat down took three very deep breaths and relaxed his shoulders. That felt good. He was ready.

34. Did The Scarecrow Move

Kate was running, her chest burning, her breathing short and far too quick. It was dark and she was unable to see the who, or the what she was escaping from. She tripped, her head clattering against the down-pipe of an old red brick wall. Water cascaded across her face and her brain was consumed by a terrible ringing sensation. She woke.

Kate grabbed the phone and set the glass she had knocked over back upright on her bedside table. She noticed the time, still only ten twenty, not too bad then.

'Sorry Ma'am.' Kate knew the voice. Bill Carter from the station.

'What's up Bill?'

'There's a big commotion going on down outside the Parklands Mosque Kate. The riot squad are there but apparently the main man causing the trouble is asking for you. It sounds like a very delicate situation.'

'The main man?'

'Yes Ma'am. Goes by the name of Imam Khalid. Mean anything to you?'

'It most certainly does Bill. I'm on my way.'

Kate dressed quickly whilst at the same time dialling for as-sistance. 'Eve? I need you.'

'No chance Kate I'm pissed.'

'Fair enough.' Kate flew out the door.

She arrived at a stand-off. A large group of Asians formed a circular barrier hiding their focus from any outside eyes. A much smaller number of officers stood alongside riot control vehicles seemingly unsure of their next actions. There was a buzz that was increasing in both intensity and hostility made more unnerving by the darkness of the night.

Kate was directed to the officer in command and introduced herself. 'Thanks for coming DI Taylor it seems you are the key to sorting this out.' This was important enough to have a senior officer on site, nobody wanted what could become a race issue messed up, it tended to destroy careers. As usual Kate's career wasn't important.

'Not sure about that but I'll give it a go Sir. Let me just give the old Imam a call.' Kate stepped to one side. 'Get Kate Taylor to sort out the contentious shit why don't you, same old, same old.' Kate was muttering to herself yet again. 'Hello Imam Khalid, it's DI Taylor. I am told you requested my appearance at your unscheduled event.'

'Yes Kate, thank you for coming. My people will let you through, I merely wish to explain our actions and then you can hopefully take over.'

'Hopefully, Khalid?'

'I'll explain please come through.'

Kate strode toward the circle of men hoping the Imam held as much sway as he seemed to think he did. On cue they parted. She followed the corridor they had created to the centre of the heaving mass. She received a plethora of inconsistent looks, some almost welcoming, others clearly threatening, most inquisitive, all directed at an infidel in their midst. There was an overwhelmingly pungent smell of sweet perfumes masking an underlying veil of musk. Kate was not scared but she was wary.

She reached the centre. Two men were prostrate on the floor

their faces bruised, lips cut and bleeding, fear and defiance taking turns to dominate their features. Above them stood the Imam.

'Imam Khalid.'

'Kate.' His voice was soft considering the tense situation they both found themselves in.

'Explain please.'

'As I am sure you know we sought to protest on Sunday against the evil in our community. We failed, we felt humiliation at the lack of support from the followers of Allah. This we could not allow to continue. We have done God's work and these pieces of shit are the result.'

'Are you saying these men are involved in the grooming of girls Khalid.'

'I am, Kate.'

'Okay, then if you would please request the crowd disperse then I will take them into custody.'

'There is one small problem Kate.'

'Always a problem' thought Kate.

'Some of those congregated here want these two men to suffer the justice of Sharia Law and you I believe you know what that means.'

Kates eyes widened in disbelief, this had suddenly become a nightmare with too many possible endings and from where she was standing none of them were good. 'Stoning?'

'Yes Kate. Stoning.'

'You have four accusers?' Kate remembered the tutorial she had received from the Imam.

'We have a thousand and four.'

Kate ignored the exaggeration and concentrated on the things that mattered. 'And how much control, are you able to assert Khalid.'

'I think we are about to find out. Just one thing Kate. If I am able to hand them over to you, will you promise this thing ends here, no repercussions.'

'I can promise you one thing Imam if you allow Sharia Law to triumph tonight you will have started something you will regret for the rest of your life.' Kate stared hard into his eyes. He blinked. She had made her point. She could do nothing more.

'So what is the situation DI Taylor.' Chief Inspector Colin Freedman had been waiting patiently and rather tentatively for Kate's return and report. He was shorter than most commanders she had come across, nearing retirement by the look of his stomach and his receding hairline. Still everything that should be polished, was polished. Kate grinned thinking that with buttons shining like that he must be good at his job.

'What's amusing DI Taylor.' Kate shook her grin from her face. She'd done it again. Never mind too late now, just ignore the question.

'Sir we may have a problem.'

'May have, DI Taylor I would have thought it was bloody obvious we do.' It was Colin Freedman's turn to grin, his head swivelling to soak up any appreciation of his comments that might be swirling in the air. There were none.

Kate sighed realising she had another one of those dickheads in front of her. 'Yes Sir, may have Sir. It all depends on whether the Imam can persuade the rabble from stoning two men to death Sir. My money says he can, just about.'

'We can't have that Taylor, certainly not. There's only one rule of law and we are here to uphold it.'

'Excellent Sir I'll be off then.' Kate was playing with fire, but she just couldn't help herself.

Chief Inspector Freedman narrowed his eyes, his nostrils flared but only momentarily. He was totally unsure how to play this, he even, for the first time in his life felt out of his depth both with the situation and with the woman in front of him. He decided he had been behind that damned desk too long. And then there was his reputation. He regained control of his thoughts. Delegation would see him through this.

'You will stay exactly where you are. It would appear you are our only link to the leaders of this debacle and as such you will have to take responsibility for what happens.'

Kate chewed her lip. 'So, do we get the batons out and charge Sir or do we wait for the Imam to prove his authority.' The mood of the crowd seemed to ebb and flow, a wave of agreement and dissent, anger and reasoning. Kate wasn't sure who was gaining the upper hand.

'That DI Taylor has to be your call.'

Not for the first time in her life Kate was being "kippered". 'Are you saying Sir, that you are handing over full control of this operation to me, Sir.'

Freedman hesitated, wondering if this could be construed as abandoning responsibility, abdication rather than delegation. He decided that if he used the right words it would not. He searched for those words.

'I am saying DI Taylor you are the only person who has access to all of the facts and that as you have previous knowledge of the ring leader you might have a better chance of "playing him" and of therefore achieving an end result that is beneficial to us all.'

'Fine Sir.' Kate reached for her phone. 'Khalid are you winning?'

'It would help Kate if you would withdraw all of your vehicles and officers from the scene, all that is, except you.'

'Are you serious?'

'Deadly Kate. Do that as an act of good faith and you will get your men.'

'Deal.' Kate turned to find Damian smiling in her face. 'Hi Ma'am Eve called me sorry I took so long to get here, needed to finish my Montego Bay. Had to brush my teeth as well always need to do that after chicken like that.'

Kate felt like hugging Damian. He always seemed to put things in perspective. 'Thanks for coming. Follow me.'

'Sir we have been requested to withdraw by the Imam. I have without your authority agreed. I and DC Lewis here, will remain. I trust that will let you off the hook Sir.'

'What did you say Taylor?'

'I said I know it's not playing it by the book Sir, but I believe it to be the correct thing to do under the circumstances. We will with the help of the Imam bring the two suspects in Sir. I take full responsibility for anything that happens from here on in, Sir.'

Colin Freedman took very little time to see the benefits this outcome presented for him and immediately began to order his force from area.

'Good luck DI Taylor I will see you back at your station.'

With the departure and much to Kate's relief the crowd began to disperse as soon as the police had left leaving only the Imam and four other men to guard their "prisoners".

'They are yours Kate.'

'I will need to call up a van for these two.'

'No Kate we will accompany you to ensure they are safely delivered to justice. I can assure you, you will have very many witnesses to their guilt, just call me when you are ready.'

'Thank you, Imam Khalid. You will certainly be getting a call following this evenings events, there will be repercussions I'm afraid. But for now, this has been a great day for common sense, and, if I may say so a wonderful day for all of our community, and I thank you. Having said that, please do not do it again.'

Ali Khalid laughed translating to his friends. Three of them laughed a fourth did not. He spoke quickly in a tone not suited to the conciliatory approach everyone else was adopting.

The Imam looked disapprovingly but translated, as he must. 'This man says, this, will certainly not happen again. He says if there is a next time, there will be a stoning.'

DI Taylor was not impressed. Two men were in custody suspected of playing a part in creating a grooming gang. It should have been the result of excellent police work, but no, it was entirely the result of mob justice. What made things worse was that recent events meant other gangs would have gone to ground, except perhaps the totally arrogant ones, whose dicks really did control their brains. 'There is hope then.' She let out a loud sigh.

On top of that there was DS Kamani's personal tragedy. They would all pay their respects, as a team. It seemed right that way. At least Eve was back. It was Rashi's awful news with which she began the meeting. She kept it short and sweet. It was necessary. Maybe not appropriate. She moved on to more pressing matters. Kate was often accused of a lack of sympathy. She begrudgingly accepted the charge.

'DC Lewis report please.' Damian had been struck dumb by the news of Rashi's father. Only yesterday they had laughed as they slid down a bank covering themselves in mud and leaves and little glory.

'Rashi and, sorry, together with DS Kamani' DC Lewis corrected himself before moving on with his report 'we worked alongside two girls previously imprisoned by Andrei Micalovic as sex slaves. These girls showed incredible bravery in entering a building, housing the man's new operation. They have done all they can for us and were able to confirm his new venture will open next Friday.'

'Just over a week to plan. Excellent work DC Lewis. Eve will you replace DS Kamani and take over this part of the investigation. Lewis update DI Kendall and let's have a nice surprise put together for the opening night. Let's add a few fireworks to the evening shall we?'

'No problem I'll get on to it straight away. Well done DC Lewis you and DS Kamani have performed brilliantly.' Eve recognised Damian's distress for his colleague and sought to lift him from it. There was even more important work to be done and they would both need to be at their best, all guns firing. There would be time for reflection later.

Kate nodded in appreciation of Eve's management of the situation. 'I can add to the good news by informing you that due to the unusual, although not particularly lawful efforts of the Muslim community, two men are in custody accused of child abuse and grooming offences.' There was a mixture of celebration and despair in Kate's voice.

'Unusual Ma'am?' Tess had her interest piqued.

'Don't ask.' Kate shook her head as the events of the previous night came back to her. She still had to face the music with DCI Freedman. That could wait.

'We seem to find ourselves on the cusp of achieving something ladies and gentlemen.' She threw a cheeky acknowledgement in Damian's direction. At one time there had been three gentlemen, how things change during the lifetime of an operation.

'I'm hoping we can gain valuable information from the two blokes in the cells and who knows, perhaps the Imam has some more to give. In a week's time we will have another crack at, what's he called, Micalovic. With luck on our side we could soon be sat here toasting success. Let's make sure we are. In the meantime, we need to maintain and even exceed our efforts to date, keep digging folks, there's still a lot of pain out there and it won't go away on its own.

35. Good Things

Jenny sighed to herself. It had been fun, but at the end of the day, Eve had been right. He was a great lad, funny, calm, down to earth and nice so very, very, nice. Not her type at all. She was tempted to change her "type" it would be so easy to do, but she was unpredictable, and that was the last thing this boy needed. She would miss his smiling face, the late nights under the sheets, behind the pub, in the shop doorways, and the Chinese, that was something else.

She loved the way he thought he knew everything. How sometimes he would treat her as being a silly girl. She rather liked that, it made her feel strangely free. He did it in a nice way, and she played the part. She would tilt her head, smile, giggle, and she would always say, "what?" But a picnic, come on. Everything comes to an end sometime. She would let him down easily.

Damian just couldn't stop grinning, he couldn't help himself. The time he had spent with her had been brilliant, a once in a lifetime experience. Jenny was just so much fun to be with. She was loud, sassy, rarely serious and she certainly had a few tricks up her sleeve when it came to it. The problem was "it came to it" anytime, anyplace, anywhere, and he was certain that sooner or later he was going to be caught in a very embarrassing situation, especially for a copper. I mean, behind the fish tank in the Chinese last night. Ridiculous.

She had an amazing laugh, and while he knew he wasn't exactly Einstein she said such stupid things. They really creased him up. It was the way she would say something daft and then say 'What?' He liked that.

But it had to stop. He wasn't getting enough sleep, he was putting on weight, and worst of all he was neglecting his family. It had to end. They could still be friends.

'For goodness sake. Somebody is having a laugh. Can't a girl have some peace.' This was the second time this morning, a Saturday morning and it was still only ten o'clock. The first call had been Jenny. As Eve had made the introduction, albeit at Jenny's request, Jenny had decided Eve would be the right person to bring it to an end. 'Crap' thought Eve. She had been about to take the required action, but now somebody else wanted a piece of her.

'Hello.' Eve's voice was abrupt. Ill tempered. A silence followed.

'Who got out of the bed on the wrong side then.' Eve recognised the chilled tones of DC Lewis. I won't keep you Eve I just need some advice.'

Eve couldn't believe this. She did not need this. 'About?'

'Jenny.'

Eve was speechless. She turned her head sideways, looked at the wall. 'Unbelievable' she muttered.

'You what?'

'Nothing, do go on.'

'It's a bit difficult what with you being her friend and all, but I really need it to stop. She's lovely, great and under different circumstances, who knows.' Eve had been nodding her head unable to comprehend how she had ended up in this pathetic crossfire.

'You're rambling Lewis.' Eve interrupted because she really didn't care. It wasn't her problem and anyway they had just solved the problem themselves. 'So you want me to tell Jenny you don't want to see her again, because you are a spineless idiot. Do I have the gist of it Lewis?'

'Sort of.'

'Consider it done.' Eve swiped the phone terminating the call, leaving Damian dangling on the other end. 'Sorted.' All she had to do was to tell each of her friends she had relayed their messages, and all would be well. Eve grabbed her toast from the grill threw it in the bin and started again. That was the last time she would be playing cupid.

36. Plucked

For DS Kendall it was a repeat performance. Little changed, only the fatalities. DC Lewis was only starting to get used to it. It was done with stealth, the world a quiet place, holding its breath before the storm. And yet the air vibrated with a cacophony of sounds. Boots scraped the floor, harnesses carelessly rattled, controlled breathing flooded the atmosphere already thick with tension and adrenaline. Small sounds, big noise, every sinew stretching, every sense reeling under pressure. And then calm.

They both loved it for different reasons. Damian, for the new-found excitement. For Eve, it was the violence, the justice, a revenge she needed to enact elsewhere and couldn't. It was a drug, an addiction, she would not soon, give up.

Eve tapped the shoulder of DC Lewis. She beckoned for him to go with her. They had their instructions, the glory, was not for them. Eve had other ideas. In the little time they had spent staking out the premises, Eve and Damian had noticed a separate entrance to the units, two blocks down from the main target, frequently being used as an exit. It might have nothing to do with Micalovic but something about the men leaving the building that way suggested it might.

If the two officers were to have some part in proceedings, when the action started, it would be there. If that was intended as an alternative escape route, a mistake had been made, and Eve, was going to reap the reward of good police work.

Damian was getting edgy, nerves tingling, hands sweating, heart thumping. Eve leant against the wall watching like a bird of prey waiting for movement from an unsuspecting victim. All around them was still, the voices of the men standing outside the entrance to the building could be easily heard, a lit cigarette providing the glow that fully confirmed their presence.

They joked. They settled into a routine that would mark their evenings for some time to come and welcomed the money that went with it.

And then the night exploded. Even though he had been expecting it Damian was taken by surprise and inadvertently stepped back on to DS Kendall's toes. 'Twat.' DC Lewis received a sharp retort and a slap across the head. It hurt but he couldn't help laughing at her reaction, it was so cool. She was fast becoming his hero.

Firearms officers stormed the building, two shocked doormen thrown to the floor before they could recover from the surprise that hit them like a sledgehammer. But this was not to be like the last encounter with Andrei Micalovic. Apart from the shouting generated for effect by the police entering the property, the random crashes and breaking of glass, the sound of overturned furniture, and the terrified screams of the hostesses, it was over before it had begun. No shots fired, no last stand just abject surrender. Figures were being herded from the club and escorted swiftly to waiting vans appearing from nowhere in front of the building. A few hobbled and one or two showed the sign of bruising or small cuts and grazes, otherwise this operation was proving to be one hell of an anti-climax.

And then the little door to their own little adventure opened, and there he was, the man himself, the one and only Andrei Micalovic. Or at least they hoped it was. DC Lewis stepped out in front of him. Andrei was cornered. He looked around for a way out. All he saw was a large police officer barring his way. He weighed his opponent up, eyes darting desperately to and fro.

'You're not big enough mate. Give up.' Damian wasn't sure about that, but he had decided it was worth the bluff.

Micalovic had to decide. One against one was probably his best odds. He snarled at DC Lewis. Damian didn't flinch, but he did grin. 'I don't mean me mate.' Andrei didn't understand. He heard the footsteps too late. 'I meant her.' His head jarred sideways, a powerfully thrown punch knocking him to the floor. He tried to rise only to receive another blow for his troubles.

Eve looked around quickly before aiming a final kick at the man she had floored. 'That felt good.' Eve's knuckles were badly grazed and her toe was now throbbing, but the pain was nothing compared to the complete and absolute pleasure she had experienced in dealing out her own brand of punishment. 'Cuff him DC Lewis, tight like. We'll drag him over to one of the vans and hand him over. He can go with all the others they seem to be collecting. It certainly turned out to be a good haul. Included in the stream of men heading for the station were some very well dressed individuals, and not a few faces that rang bells with many of the officers. There would be major content for the newspapers and complete embarrassment for some of the club's customers. The problem was going to be, would the girls talk?

'DC Lewis leaned against one of the police vehicles catching his breath, letting his blood pressure ease whilst DI Kendall completed her retelling of the action to the senior operation's officer. The two of them would get no credit for this, but they knew what they had just done, and that's what mattered right now.

Two figures being bundled into a van close by caught Damian's attention. His heart sank. Two girls swearing and shrieking abuse at the officers escorting them, kicking and spitting, drunk or drugged. He fought hard to control the tears as the van door closed and sped off, Irena and Katya part of its human cargo.

'We meet again Mr Micalovic.' Eve enjoyed the greeting although she couldn't put her finger on which Bond film it reminded her of. She was also grateful she hadn't been tempted to use a foreign accent. That might not have sounded quite right on the tape running in the background.

Andrei Micalovic eyed the woman who had addressed him. He said nothing but his looks revealed his feelings. His head still hurt.

'I presume you are aware we found the body of your friend.' Another nail in his coffin that looked likely to be buried deep.

'How did he die Mr Micalovic.' It was Kate's turn to delve.

The man sat back in his hard, wooden chair unperturbed.

'Trafficking, prostitution, child abuse and murder, probably more, but let's start with those shall we.' His attitude was annoying Kate. He was holding something back, he was too confident, appeared to be biding his time.

'So where would you like to start Mr Micalovic.'

'Let's go straight to the end.' Finally, he was making his move. He certainly seemed to think his statement was extremely clever if the smile on his face was anything to go by.

'The end Mr Micalovic is a long time in prison.'

'You are wrong. The end is my freedom.'

'Well that's a conversation stopper' thought Eve. She leaned menacingly toward the table. 'Did I really hit you that hard because your brain is certainly not working.'

'Please be so good as to explain yourself Mr Micalovic.' Kate was intrigued not so much as to what this man might have to say but by his arrogance. She also had to admit the man had a weird and clearly evil sort of charisma. A snake came to mind.

'I am just a small fish. You stick me in prison and that's that. I can offer you much more I think.'

'Please continue.'

Micalovic let out a slow sigh. 'No. I don't think so. First a deal. I give you an important catch and you send me home, deport me if you like, no charges.'

'Sorry no deals.' Kate followed the official line knowing full well common sense would prevail if what Micalovic was saying was true.

'Then lock me up, but the real criminal, the man you really want, will simply replace me, and the crimes you describe will in a short time continue, just as before.'

'You will have to give me so much more before I can even start to consider your proposal.'

'The man I am talking about is a thorn in your side.'

Now that was interesting. She hoped for a fleeting moment it was Ratcliffe, her smile betrayed her thoughts. He was very convincing, absolutely certain the name he was withholding would be of note. Kate glanced at Eve, they had to know. A deal would be offered. It could always be withdrawn, the wording used ambiguous, the result unexpected for some.

'Ok Mr Micalovic, tell me more, lead us to this man who you consider to be such an important individual and we will send you home.'

'Put it in writing.'

'It's on tape that will have to do.'

'I have your word.'

'Absolutely.' A clever man would have read something in Kate's face. This man didn't.

'His name is Saad Hassan.'

Kate swallowed but managed to keep a poker face. Eve spluttered before speaking. 'The local councillor?'

'The same.'

'Just words Mr Micalovic.' Kate had recovered from the surprise of his revelation. 'I'm afraid we will need something more substantial.' She was pushing it but Micalovic had laid his cards on the table, there was nothing to lose.

'I cannot give you anything that might be possibly turned against me, something about my completely legal operations that you might consider gives some, truth, to your allegations. However, I can perhaps pass on some information about his dealings that have nothing to do with me.' His eyes twinkled, he was enjoying himself, sat there with his arms crossed, slumped lazily in his chair, legs out straight before him. Kate would let him savour the moment knowing her turn would come.

'We can sit here all day if you like but save us the theatrics and just tell us what you know.' Kate was bursting inside to know what Micalovic had on Hassan. That bastard had caused so much trouble for the force, pulled so many strings to get clearly guilty child abusers back on the streets. She found she wanted him even more than she wanted the man in front of her. Inside she knew she would have both.

'Saad Hassan will have gone to ground. He will reappear in the not too distant future because he is driven by the money operations like those you have destroyed can bring. But he also has an itch that he cannot help himself from scratching.'

Eve shifted impatiently in her seat wondering which part of saving the "theatrics" he had failed to understand. Okay he was helping but she found him odious, she hated the smirk, the air of superiority that was growing by the minute. She so desperately wanted to slap him again.

Micalovic suspected he had his audience where he wanted them, despite what the well-practised looks on their faces was suggesting. Kate leant forward, her hands resting on the table, bearing witness to her interest was the pale skin on her knuckles. Her continual restlessness told of her desire for information, but he was becoming bored and home beckoned.

'Saad Hassan is a highly active member of what you call

grooming gangs and I can tell you where he satisfies his perverted desires.'

Kate had not expected self-righteousness to be a part of the man's faults, but he never ceased to amaze, she would give him that. Eve pushed the pen and paper already provided across the table. 'Write it down.'

'And I go home?'

'Oh yes,' said DI Taylor.

Kate rose, declared the interview at an end and ushered Eve outside. Micalovic set about his task while the guards waited to return him to his cell. Tonight, he would dream of freedom, of home.

Kate marched straight to the coffee machine before they returned to her office. 'Bloody hell Eve, Saad Hassan.'

37. Crow Power

This could not be happening. It wasn't funny. In actual fact it was bloody serious. Four words played in a continuous loop through her head. "This won't happen again."

'Sarge tell me it's not true.'

'Wish I could Ma'am.' Bill Carter raised his eyebrows in sympathy with the angry woman in front of him. 'Happened this afternoon while you were out. Didn't think you would be best pleased.'

'Who authorised it Bill?'

'Came from the top Kate. It was one of those no questions asked moments. Seems to me they happen a bit too regularly for this type of crime.'

Kate felt like smashing something, anything but then her cynical side clicked in.

'You know what Bill the chances of us cutting through the political shit and getting a conviction were probably small. This way the bastards are, I think, going to get what they deserve.'

Bill Carter was confused. 'Haven't they just got up and walked away with what was due to them Kate.'

'Out of the frying pan into the fire Bill, and believe me, it's a bloody hot fire. I'm pretty damn sure they will get what they deserve.'

Sergeant Carter watched her go wandering what she had meant. Kate continued with her thoughts as she walked. What was done was done, a certain kind of justice, like it or not. It could probably be counted as a result and she was closing the case on those two poor buggers. She had Andrei Micalovic's much larger fish to fry.

Two men laughed as they stumbled along the pavement. They had been drinking. It was forbidden. They talked of sex, of white trash. They had been sentenced. Justice had not been administered. Their presence humiliated their community, disgraced their religion.

They would continue along their well-worn path. They would pick up where they had left off, not so long ago. They believed themselves untouchable. Fate would decree they were wrong.

Two men stumbling along the pavement never reached their intended destination. Their bodies were not found. If they had been, they would have borne witness to their demise, they would be evidence of another law, their law. No one mourned.

She had arranged to meet the whole team. They had been watching the movements of Saad Hassan and they were almost certain today would see him behind bars, although they could not be certain for how long. If nothing else they could certainly put a stain on his reputation, however scant a punishment this would be for his evil acts.

The information given by Micalovic had identified a house in Roche. It was a large detached house set in a secluded garden, well kept lawns on three sides, flower beds adding a variety of colour to the surroundings . This had surprised Kate she had expected something else. They had kept eyes on the property for several days and noticed the regular visits of both young girls and older men who strode purposefully up the short drive and in to the building. Hassan hadn't shown, and they had stayed their hand. It troubled them but the prize was huge. For Kate it was the only prize. Today the good news was the sight of Hassan's car parked in the drive. 'Got you, you bastard.' Kate winked at DS Kendall.

They all knew their remit. They were not supposed to do the exciting stuff, the dirty work like the raid they were about to undertake, but they all wanted this badly, they craved it and they were going in. This was their gig and they would enjoy every minute.

'DC Lewis you and Campbell cover the front. Keep him from his car. DS Kendall and I will go around the back and make a grand entrance. I fully expect him to bolt so be ready. Remember two objectives. Apprehend Saad Hassan and detain as many witnesses as possible. I'm not exactly expecting a Who's Who of Loxborough because this looks like a low end of the market set up, but we might find men who will talk.'

Kate Taylor and Eve disappeared around the side of the house. Damian and Tess approached Hassan's car slowly but purposefully.

'I've an idea.' Tess Campbell looked mischievous. She moved to the metre wide patch of earth alongside the large privet hedge that surrounded the garden. She returned with a lethal looking gardening fork.

'What the hell is that for, expecting trouble?'

'Not particularly.' Tess rammed the fork into the rubber of the car's front tyre, took two steps backwards and slashed again at the rear tyre. 'That should stop him.'

'Let's hope it is his car and he is bloody guilty of something or we have just committed the crime of vandalism, and boy are we going to look stupid or what.'

'What are you two doing?' The booming voice of a muscle bound, suited and booted gorilla rushed toward him, a similarly sized and more informally dressed ape behind him.

'Bloody hell, bouncers' cried Damian.

'Police stay where you are.' Tess shouted in panic her voice reedy and lacking the necessary authority to stop a couple of rhinos bent on destruction. Damian was floored with a sledge hammer of a punch, his attacker brushing past before grabbing DC Campbell and smashing her against the car. She reacted quickly kneeing him but missing her mark. This merely succeeded in making him even angrier. He picked her up and bodily threw her into to the thick branches of the hedge. She bounced sickeningly back, crashing to the floor where her head collided with the asphalt and she lay unmoving, blood seeping from her forehead.

Damian had been stunned but the sight of Tess being thrown around like a rag doll brought his usually unseen temper to the boil. He had taken a few more punches from the second brute but they had merely served to heighten his senses, Damian began to see everything in slow motion. He grabbed his assailant by the balls and squeezed tight bringing him to his knees. Two of his fingers sunk into the man's rapidly tear filing eyes, temporarily blinding him and leaving him open to Damian's revenge. Two savage stamps. Two broken legs. The man a shuffling wreck. The sheer brutality of the young police officers assault brought his mate to a halt. He circled warily.

A cry rang out. 'Where are you? Hurry up get the bloody car going.' Damian's would be assailant froze his attention distracted for a precious moment that left him prey to an anger, Damian had not felt, for a very long time. Seconds later the second minder collapsed to the floor, pain flooding his brain. Another leg shattered under the weight of Damian's boot.

'Don't bloody move.'

Damian looked up. Just a few metres away stood Saad Hassan. Very recent events suggested this was not much of a concern for the marauding officer. The gun in Hassan's hand said otherwise.

'Don't do anything stupid.' DC Lewis was now calm. It was

time for talking. 'You're not going anywhere it's over. Put your gun down and everything will be okay.'

'That's not going to happen and if you don't get out of my way, I will shoot you, make no mistake about that.'

'You're the one who has made the mistake Hassan.' Damian's shoulders relaxed, the relief on his face palpable. It wasn't over yet, but Kate was there, and he felt strangely secure. She and Eve had strolled into the house through the back door causing nothing more than a temporary stir, a confused halt in proceedings. Eve's booming orders had sent the men to their knees while the more enterprising girls looked for escape. Both Kate and Eve were disappointed in the wholesale submission, they had looked forward to cracking some heads. Kate had heard the sounds of violence from the front of the house and had arrived it would seem at just about the right time.

'You have nothing on me. Nobody in there is going to accuse me of anything. This is just another racist attempt to destroy the reputation of an honest man, a great servant of the community.'

'You might be right Hassan.' Maybe those inside won't talk. Your problem is you are pointing a gun at a police officer. That will do for me, that, and the testimony of Andrei Micalovic.' Kate's words stunned Hassan. His nerves began to unravel and along with them his good sense.

He looked at Damian and sighed, anger flashing in his eyes. Without warning he turned, swiftly aiming his gun at the officer behind him. Damian moved quicker than he knew he could. Diving forward he smashed Hassan to the ground. It was too late. The gun fired and DI Taylor collapsed in a heap on the floor. Lewis had time to render Hassan unconscious with an elbow to the head before shrieking at Kate. 'Kate, Ma'am.' He was horrified as Kate's body lay limp on the floor. Kate was also horrified, she had slipped at a vital moment and was feeling totally embarrassed.

'Don't worry Lewis I'm fine. Managed to dodge it, near miss.'

Damian loomed above her and helped her to her feet. 'I'm so glad you're okay. Where's DS Kendall?' DC Lewis regarded Kate with an expression of total awe and respect wondering how she had acted quick enough to dodge a bullet.

'I left her to round up the witnesses. We've locked all the doors so they can only get out through the front. You clean up here. Borrow my cuffs and I'll go and help DI Kendall.' Kate was about to leave when she realised there was something missing. 'Where's DC Campbell?'

Lewis was already by her side cradling her head gently. 'Is she okay Lewis?'

'No Ma'am call an ambulance quickly.' Kate ran over. DC Campbell was unconscious her face a mess, her right arm hanging awkwardly. 'That bastard is going to pay for this.' Kate looked at DC Lewis. He had changed. Today had aged him, matured him, made him a real copper. Kate liked the change. Lewis might not.

'Stay with her. I'll sort these three out, and then I'll join Eve.'

The three men cursing the day they had underestimated a young police officer were collected within minutes of the call reaching the station Saad Hassan was unceremoniously bundled off for processing, the other two helped to an ambulance and taken for repairs. Seven more men followed, heads bowed, feet shuffling. A small number of female officers guided half a dozen girls to police vehicles. another set of victims of what seemed to be an insatiable lust for young flesh. Kate stood alongside Eve watching the comings and goings the aftermath of a violent afternoon.

'What's the next step Ma'am.'

'To be honest I don't know DS Kendall. I'm afraid it could well be our last throw of the dice, only time and politics will decide.'

The night was still comparatively young when Kate and Eve finally completed the paperwork. Damian had accompanied Tess to the hospital. His phone call had been positive. Tess had sustained severe injuries, but a full recovery was expected, although not in the very immediate future. It had been a long, exciting, disturbing, and for some very painful day. Perhaps tomorrow would give some indication of how successful or not it had been.

38. Always Expect

Her glass was half empty. She liked it that way. Italian Barolo. Expensive. She remembered how it had started. She felt the shower cascading over her shoulders, her stomach, her legs. She would indulge herself again later. If she recalled correctly it was a sausage roll and a Pepsi. She preferred tonight's menu, red wine and Fettuccini Alfredo, Roman style. Unlike the last time she wouldn't have to dress to impress in the morning. Let it all hang out. She would have a hangover, dead certainty, but there would be no important meeting no bullshit to listen to.

Had that meeting an eternity ago been important? What had she achieved? Apart from the taking down of Andrei Micalovic. There was Saad Hassan. Attempted murder. Brilliant. Wasn't what they had signed up to though. That part was a disaster. She considered events. It had been like a bloody game show. Put them in prison let them out. Wash rinse repeat. The politics involved when those poor young girls were being raped, beaten, drugged, passed around like toys and left to rot like carrion fodder.

She was getting morbid. It was the drink. She topped her glass up. What else. When a drink or two was involved in the privacy of her home Kate inevitably began to talk to herself. 'Trent Kruse. He's dead.' Kate nodded solemnly. 'DC Campbell she will be laid up for a while'. Kate reflected on that one. 'She'll survive and prosper her type always do. There must be more. Hold on, that wasn't fair about Tess, she did do some things right. "Everybody can do something good". Who said that, some genius, no I know, Colonel Sanders.' Kate chuckled and then frowned, desperately trying to bring back memories from the not so distant past. 'Murders. Solved two. Nice one. Saad Hassan got him. Said that already.' Things were getting difficult to recall now, her eyelids were heavy, the shower might have to wait. She drifted and woke with a start. Jewellery shop, don't forget the jewellery shop. Bloody Damian. Idiot.

'We saved those girls. Did we though.' Kate thought about it. 'Doubt it, probably back on the street.' The arm holding up her chin collapsed frightening her back to consciousness.
'Grooming gangs? Didn't catch a single one. Kate Taylor, you are a waste of space.'

She woke with a start. It seemed so much colder. A draught spread around her ankles. A shadow moved. Silly, just her imagination. 'Hello DI Taylor.' The words were spoken with menace, sprinkled with evil intent by a partially hidden figure.' It stepped forward.

'What the...' Kate's words were cut short. The blow knocked her from her chair. Everything went black.

Cold water dragged her back to her senses and there, standing before her, was Frank Moon. So, he had finally turned up although not quite as expected. He had taken his time, but he had come. 'How did you get in Frank?' She was using her professional guile, her training was doing the talking, it came naturally. Be nice until it gets dirty, that was the name of the game. And that's exactly what it was, one of life's little games, games that Kate made a habit of winning, only this time she was taped to a chair, and her luck was running thin. Her experience told her there was always hope, and there was always Kenny, he had promised. What she needed was time.

'It was easy.' Frank Moon spoke for the first time. Kate had experience of how these guys loved to brag, how they loved to tell you how clever they were. 'You made it so simple by getting yourself pissed. I thought I would to have to smash the door down, but you, Miss clever bloody detective, left the frigging door open, I couldn't believe my luck.'

'So Frank, what's your plan?'

'I'm just going to take my time, enjoy making you suffer, enjoy a nice bit of revenge for all that time I spent locked up, all because of you.' His voice was rising, his fists clenching. He stopped and took a deep intake of air. It calmed him down. 'I'm obviously going to kill you and here's the good bit.' He produced a syringe and placed it on the table next to Kate. 'I'm going to stick this in you. Far too much stuff in there of course. Ironic isn't it.'

'Yes Frank it is. Very good. Mind you, you have had a lot of time to think about it haven't you. Must say credit where it's due, it does look nice and clean.'

'I can soon change that.'

This was going nowhere it was becoming a childish standoff, and that, wasn't good. She had to get him back on track but how long could she keep him there. Kate's thoughts drifted. If a knight in shining armour was going to come to her rescue, he was certainly taking his time. She had to cling to the very slight hope that Kenny would come. He had promised her he would have her back. He was not a man to let you down. She could rely on his word. Reality hit her in the form of a backhanded slap from Moon. 'You aren't listening.' He was right and that was an amateurish mistake. Never antagonise.

And then there it was. Frank Moon's snarling made him oblivious to it. Kate's faith in her friend meant she saw it. A small red dot flicked around the room. For a fleet second it came within inches of Moon's head. The angle was wrong.

She looked at her captor. His lips curled back over his teeth and he dribbled down the side of his mouth. His eyed were blood-shot, his face flaked with white specks of skin and his hair hung lank across his face. He shook a long menacing knife in her face more theatrics than intent. Her heart turned to ice. It was time to get dirty.

'You moron Moon.'

He slapped her again, harder, causing blood to drip from her nose.

'You've left the curtains open dickhead. Anyone can see you. You're thicker than I thought.'

'If you're so bloody clever why were you stupid enough to tell me that.'

Kate slumped, looked dejected, sighed. 'You're right about that Frank. Stupid. Too much of the red stuff.'

He laughed at her and walked over to the window. Frank Moon placed the blade of his knife between his teeth and raised his arms to draw the curtains. The red dot danced on his face, glass shattered, blood trickled down his forehead, more burst from the back of his head. A second thud, his chest cracked, a third, as his body hit the ground.

DSI Kenny Turner was the first through the door followed by a swarm of highly protected, brutally armed officers. Kate smiled through swollen lips, her eye throbbing with pain, her heart thumping with relief. 'Why is it always the last minute with you, stop for a quick half did we?'

'Almost didn't bother Kate, there was quite a good karaoke going on and it was my turn next.'

'In that case, sorry to disturb your fun. Pass the wine will you and have one yourself.'

Kenny Turner cut through the tape restraining Kate's hands. She wrung the blood back into her wrists and fingers, grasped the glass offered to her and raised it to her colleague. 'Here's to the next time.'

Kenny looked at his wine. He was tempted. Maybe later. 'Bound to be one Kate.'

39. A Slice Of Crow Pie

'What do you think Eve?' She cast her eyes over the charge sheets DI Taylor had pushed toward her. Seven men were listed, their recent catch, all living within a twenty mile radius of Loxborough. All from what might be called the "better areas" surrounding the town.

'It's not what I expected. I have to confess, it's not what we were looking for.' Eve stared for a moment at her boss. 'I have to ask Kate?'

'As it happens, I had a tussle with a mad deranged drug dealer last night. He spilt my wine and I became a bit over excited.'

'Okay Kate let me know what really happened later. These reports have me well and truly stumped.

'Exactly these are not the scruffy, dirty old men we have heard about. So, what have we stumbled into? These guys are just below the elite of this town and to be fair the girls weren't street urchins either.'

The raid they had carried out was producing more questions than answers and as the witnesses weren't talking, they had little chance of convictions. Of course, they did have Hassan, bang to rights with his pistol pulling nonsense. That on its own was a nice result. The others would go free, so where did Kate and her team go now.

Their thoughts were disturbed by a knock on the door. Sergeant Carter stepped in. 'Ma'am, DS Kendall.' He nodded at Eve. 'I thought you might like to know the phones are ringing.'

Kate viewed him questioningly and couldn't help the sarcastic response. 'Well don't ask me to come down and answer them Sergeant. What about you Eve do you have a spare moment to cover the desk for good old Sergeant Bill Carter here so he can put his poor feet up and enjoy his tenth cuppa of the day?'

Eve's look was enough to confirm she did not.

'Very funny Ma'am. I haven't laughed so much since Morecombe and Wise did their kitchen sketch. I suppose since you don't want to talk to a bunch of women claiming they were gang raped when they were young, I might as well tell them you are too busy to be bothered by such unimportant, what shall I call it Ma'am "tittle tattle".

He had their attention. 'Careful Sergeant. I apologise for any aspersions I may have cast. Right spit it out.'

It had started with one call, become a trickle and then a flood. Bill Carter had taken the first of them, heard the first tentative, emotionally charged voice, the one that finally broke the dam of fear, the wall of silence.

'It seems Ma'am your latest shenanigans may have achieved more than you thought. It appears all this has been going on for an exceedingly long time. The calls we are getting are from women in their twenties and thirties.'

'What?' The shock in Kate's voice was loud and clear. 'I don't understand Bill. How's that possible and why are they contacting us now.'

'They are contacting us now Ma'am because you have the man who was behind their misery locked up behind bars and charged with attempted murder of a police officer. Clearly, they now feel they can add to his misery without fear of any reprisal, because all of them are naming Saad Hassan. It seems Ma'am...'

'Oh, do drop the Ma'am, Bill.'

Sergeant Carter tried again. 'It seems Kate he used to be the "King of Grooming Gangs" and he was aided and abetted by one or two of the other buggers you picked up.'

'I love you Bill Carter and don't let anyone tell you anything different.'

'That might explain what we couldn't understand about the setup we smashed.' Eve's mind was racing. 'It would seem he has risen from the gutter, and now prefers more salubrious surroundings for his disgusting habits. How long might this have been going on. It's horrendous.'

'It certainly has a comparison with what happened between him and Micalovic, a dirty warehouse to a virtual saloon. Time to get busy Eve. I've a feeling we are going to need a posse to round up a very large number of bad guys once we get talking to these brave, forgotten women and I can't wait.'

They had been right. One horrific story after another was repeated to Kate and her team. It took a while, the women who came forward were severely affected by their experiences. They had hidden their horror, some called it shame for years, believing they would never be listened to. Some had spoken out before, and had been ridiculed, labelled troublemakers, and racists, but now their nightmares were at an end.

The women's stories put pressure on many of the men apprehended during the recent operation that had led to Hassan's demise. They had believed until now they would walk out the door. One or two were implicated in Hassan's earlier career and would lose their freedom. Others fearing for their reputation folded under pressure and produced new leads, more names of gangs, their members, and their locations.

Three weeks after the first of the women's phone calls, night time raids took place across Loxborough. Fifty seven men were arrested. The sheer scale of the abuse was difficult to comprehend, and yet this, was only the beginning, the tip of the proverbial iceberg.

Kate had a short time to go over her report and she wasn't enjoying it. As always, at times like this, the air vibrated to the sound of her phone. 'Every bloody time.' Thought Kate. The voice on the end was snappy, short, quick to the point, matter of fact.

'Shit.' DI Taylor collected her paperwork, placed it in her shoulder bag and popped it under her arm. She composed herself for what she had to do. Stepping from her office she stopped beside the desk of Eve Kendall.

'I'm sorry Eve.' She wanted to end her news right there. She couldn't. 'Terry Frost is dead.'

Eve's face went white, her body sagged, her hands shook.

'I've only just been told Eve, a short phone call but it seems it was the result of a mixed message, Chinese whispers. When he arrived at the prison a few of the prisoners heard he was a paedophile not a paedo killer. He took a beating, didn't recover.' Kate didn't wait. She couldn't, there were too many issues here.

Eve struggled to make it to the washrooms, picked a cubicle, sat down, and sobbed like she had not done for a very long time. The next few days would be a gap in her memory, the Kings Arms the richer for it, the world less so.

It felt like a very lonely place to be right now on this short journey to the fourth floor. It really didn't seem that long ago that she had made her first visit to Ratcliffe's office. It had certainly been a helter skelter ride. How could such a short space of time alter so many lives. It wouldn't alter hers, she would just move on, oblivious to those above and below. Perhaps a few of those left bleeding on the side might receive a moments consideration. That's the way it was, the way it had to be. Old Will Shakespeare had it right. "All the world's a stage and men and women merely players' words from "As You Like it" thought Kate 'and I bloody well don't.'

Ratcliffe was waiting. Of course he was. Patricia was being efficient. It's what she did.

'Come in DI Taylor. Thank you Patricia.' Two women, a different face for each of them.

'Well Kate, I would like to thank you.'

'You bloody well won't though, will you,' thought Kate.

'I'll cut to the chase DI Taylor. It's over. Her thoughts had been confirmed.

'The team has achieved as much as I think it can. You and your team have had some good results DI Taylor. Caused a few more ripples than I would have liked, but you can't have everything. You Kate will be returning to Drugs and your old boss DCI Turner will be here soon to outline your new role.

'The department have taken a great deal of credit and we should all be proud of that.' Ratcliffe had embarked on a meaningless speech. Kate and her team had fought their way through shit. They all knew where the credit was going, and it wasn't in their direction.

'Any awards going begging Sir?' Kate was tired, beyond caring, people had died for the cause, the men behind desks, the living, would get the applause.

'Sorry?'

'Di Trent Kruse he died Sir, Remember? DC Tess Campbell severely injured Sir, DS Eve Kendall went through hell Sir. Any awards in the offing, Sir?'

'All unfortunate Kate. Rest assured the parts they played will be remembered.'

Kate looked at her superior officer with disbelief in her eyes 'Oh just fuck off Sir.'

'I beg your pardon Di Taylor.'

Kate had gone too far, and she knew it. Attitude was one thing, stupidity another. An apology was due, she was aware of that, but could she make it? Her problem disappeared as the door opened. Kenny Turner had arrived on the scene, yet another of his very much appreciated interventions.

'Hi guys am I late.'

'No Kenny right on time.' Kate smiled at her mentor. He knew her well enough to know there was a bit more to Kate's enthusiastic welcome. He nodded at her, a telepathic understanding passing between them.

'Have you told Kate what's happening Jon?'

'I was just about to.' DCS Ratcliffe was about to be rid of this woman, he didn't need to take things further. 'DI Taylor we are changing the remit of your team. From today it will be a community service based operation. As I said you will be moving back to your old job, but I am sure there are a couple of your team you might like to recommend to carry on the work they have been doing to such good effect.'

There it was then. She felt relieved, sad, pleased, unfulfilled, ready. 'Community based Sir?'

'Yes DI Taylor, I think there has been enough division.'

Kate chewed her lip. 'Not much left of my team Sir.' She hated the idea of recommending anyone to the fate Ratcliffe would impose on the members of any new "team", but she would never give a negative impression of any of them. She had to respond. If she was going to condemn her colleagues to life in the slow lane, she would at least try to get something out of it for them. And then she thought of Rashi. This might actually work for him, give him some flexibility, maybe if she played it right some extra money in his pocket. God knows he needed some of both.

'You could promote DS Kamani to lead the group Sir and DC Campbell would be a good support.'

'Promote him DI Taylor?'

'Yes Sir. Operations are always seen as successful if somebody is promoted Sir, and I would suggest he is the right one for the accolade Sir, ethnicity and all.'

Ratcliffe clearly liked the idea. Without speaking he made a note on his nice leather bound, pad. 'We'll see about that. I'm afraid we have other things in mind for DC Campbell Kate. She has certainly proved her worth to us throughout your entire operation.' Ratcliffe had suddenly come to life. 'And I do mean "entire" DI Taylor.' His face was one of complete triumph.

Kate was genuinely shocked. Had Tess Campbell played her? Impossible. Ratcliffe's face told a different story. Life sucks thought Kate. She regained her composure.

'What about the other chap. What's his name? Lewis?'

'Too good for you' thought Kate. She had no intention of letting them put Damian Lewis in a box and forgetting about him, but again she had to give positive feedback. 'He won't let you down Sir.'

'Good I'll consider your suggestions.' Over to you Ken.

'It'll be good to have you back Kate, we've missed you.' Ken Turner smiled, DCS Ratcliffe sneered. Kate took advantage.

'Thanks Sir. It will be a pleasure to work with professionals again.'

Ken Turner was used to Kate. He tried not to show his amusement. 'Kate there's a new drug on the street, bloody lethal with the wrong mix. We've a couple of our chaps undercover making progress and that's where you come in. Small team, a hub for them to report to, support for them Kate, their lives in your hands.

'How small Sir?'

'Three of you.'

'My choice Sir.'

'Totally Kate.'

'You'll have their names before we leave Sir.' She laughed. Too loud. She realised the sound was a bit manic. The faces of the two senior officers looked rather unsettled. It was childish but she didn't care.

She was content, she would be back doing what she loved, and she had every intention of saving DC Lewis from her ex-Boss, and, when the time was right, Eve Kendall would also be getting a call. Kate was back on top.

Ken Turner and Kate Taylor left the office, old comrades in crime, reunited. Jon Ratcliffe called Patricia Jennings into his room. 'You look harassed Jon.'

'That's one word for it.'

'Let me see if I can comfort you.'

Kate stopped. 'Sorry Kenny I must have left my car keys in Ratcliffe's office. I'm always leaving them behind. I've a habit of dangling them in my hands and then just putting them down and forgetting them.'

'No problem Kate see you later.'

DI Taylor returned to Ratcliffe's suite. There was no sign of Pat, just rather unusual sounds coming from Ratcliffe's office. She peered round his door. This was going to be sweet. 'Knock, Knock Sir.'

Patricia was thrown from her boss' lap and landed heavily on the floor. Kate was creasing up inside, determined not to laugh in case she couldn't stop. 'Keys Sir, forgot my keys.' Kate leaned forward and collected her keys from the desk, while a bright red, extremely ruffled senior police officer remained cemented to his chair. Kate looked at the figure languishing on the floor. 'Hi Pat.' She whispered the words as if she was witnessing the most natural thing in the world. Ratcliffe was fuming, he wanted to rant at DI Taylor but was astute enough to know when not to start digging holes.

Kate swivelled and made for the door, but before she left, she turned again. She looked at Ratcliffe, tapped her nose and winked. 'Safe with me Sir.' It had all been worthwhile after all.

She had one more thing to do and it was going to be a pleasure. The case had taken longer than expected, but the result was the one they craved. It seemed he might have walked free. Witnesses wouldn't talk or had melted into the shadier side of life. Those caught with their trousers down claimed it was a Stag Night. Ironically, it was the murder of his friend Adi Petrovic that finally convicted him. DNA, fingerprints, Adi's body became the route map to prison for Andrei Micalovic. Kate was consumed by a feeling of total triumph as she walked toward cell number 127A flanked by two large security guards, another just behind.

Inside the small but clean room a man diminished from the person he had been a few months before, stripped of his cockiness, bereft of his hope, sat on the prison bed. He looked up. Before the look would have oozed menace, today it was one that might almost be taken as disappointment.

'You lied.' A simple statement aimed at Kate Taylor. Andrei Macalovic had been found guilty as charged and duly sentenced.

'How so Mr Micalovic?'

'You promised I would be free to go home.'

'And you are. Perhaps you should listen again to the tape of our interview. You, as promised are going home and you will serve your sentence in your country. You fly tomorrow. I made a promise to all those girls whose lives you ruined. I always keep my promises Mr Micalovic.' His head dropped, his chin resting on his chest. Kate turned away from him and as she reached the door Andrei Micalovic looked up.

'Ai câştigat Kate Taylor.'

She turned toward him an inquisitive look on her face.

'You won.'

Kate Taylor nodded appreciatively to herself. He was right, she had won, and Kate would be the first to admit, she absolutely loved winning.

COMING SOON

If you have enjoyed the first in the Kate Taylor series look out for the next episode later in the year when Kate and Eve return to take on the drug gangs of Loxborough.